BEAUTY IN THE BEAST

Emily-Jane Hills Orford

Beauty in the Beast by Emily-Jane Hills Orford

Beauty in the Beast © 2022 Emily-Jane Hills Orford TXu 2-298-

734 Tell-Tale Publishing Group, Swartz Creek, MI 48437

Printed in The United States of America

CHAPTER ONE

"Amell," she screamed. "Amell. Help me."

She was pinned in a hunk of metal, the world around her growing darker by the minute. And it was cold. Bitter. Bone-chilling. A soft tongue licked her cheek. Whines and a warm breath slipped into her ear. Bear. Her three-year-old mutt, a Border Collie-Black Lab mix. Black and white. Full of love and mischief. Her strength in a time of need. Like right now.

She had rescued Bear. A puppy tossed in a dumpster. Left to die. The two were inseparable. Now, she was failing Bear. And they would die.

One final scream, "Amell."

"I'm so sorry, Bear," she whispered.

As she slipped into oblivion, she felt a fog of confusion slither through her brain. *Who is Amell?*

CHAPTER TWO

Two weeks earlier

"You can't be serious." Samantha was intent on stirring her tea. Although she claimed to be a health nut, when it came to tea, herbal or standard, she always added two sugar cubes and at least a teaspoon of milk (sometimes cream, if the mood demanded). Today it was herbal tea. Chamomile. Which, in Priya's point of view, should be taken clear. Sugar and milk would only cloud the taste and dull the soothing effects of the chamomile. She always believed in pure tea; if you wanted milk and sugar, warm up a mug of milk with sugar added. In other words, don't spoil the tea.

Priya was enjoying her favorite apple spice tea, a specialty at the tearoom the two ladies frequented in downtown Victoria. Situated on the harbor, overlooking the incoming boat traffic and the majestic Empress Hotel, which also served tea, primarily the English versions like Earl Grey, the two shared their favorite table by the window, soaking in the view.

Priya never tired of the beauty of Victoria. Even the sodden rainy days boasted a distinctly elegant ambiance. But she couldn't afford to live here anymore. Her job at the archives, a contract position, terminated in a few days. Without a steady income, with the rising cost of rent and essentials, she figured she'd last a month before she was cast onto the street. Not a pleasant thought.

"I have to live somewhere, Sammy," she used the quaint pet name, the one only she was allowed to use. Samantha cringed every time Priya called her Sammy, but she put up with it, if only to maintain their cherished friendship. "It's a job. In my field. Cataloguing and preserving books and artifacts. And it pays much better than the one at the archives. Plus, rent and food are included. It's a dream job, Sammy. I have to take it."

The waitress stopped by the table to leave a tray of oven-fresh scones and a dish of homemade strawberry jam. Priya thanked her with a smile before slipping a scone from the platter onto her plate and cutting it open carefully to allow the steam to waft up to her nostrils. The two ladies were in a somber mood, in spite of the charming setting and a table cluttered with favorite foods. It would be their last tea event, at least for a while.

"But it's so far away," Samantha argued. "So isolated. And I can't come visit you and you can't leave to visit me. For a whole year. Sounds more like a prison than an oasis in the storm."

All Samantha said was true. It was far away. High up and deep within the Boundary Range mountains. Castle Mutasim, an Arabic name for refuge. *Why Arabic?* Priya had no idea, considering British Columbia was at least halfway around the world from any Arab countries. But, with globalization, there were people of all ethnic backgrounds everywhere. Not the least in British Columbia.

"I've packed up," Priya buttered the scone, added some jam and took a bite, closing her eyes as she savored the moment. "My last day is Friday. I'm ready to load the car first thing early Saturday morning. I don't have much. Mostly memorabilia, clothes and, of course, my BFF, next to you, of course." She was referring to her rescued dog, Bear.

"Bear," Samantha finished Priya's thought. "Never did understand why you'd call the mangy mutt Bear."

"He might be a mutt, but he's not mangy," Priya stated her defense. She had been dumping her trash in the dumpster behind the apartment building when she heard the whimper. Taking a deep breath to ward off the stench, and voraciously swatting away the flies, she had bravely peaked inside. Half submerged in the mucky trash was the cutest bundle of black and white. Noticing his audience, the bundle wiggled around, thrashing and whining in hopes of a rescue. Which came immediately.

Priya, always a softie, reached into the trash and cradled the bundle in her hands, lifting him out of his garbage strewn prison. "There, there, little one. How did you end up in here? I suppose someone dumped you, didn't they? How could they? You're so adorable?" She had cooed and snuggled the smelly mutt close to her, taking it back to the apartment where she washed it in the bathtub. The mutt wasn't thrilled with the water, but it endured the procedure, giving a great shake when lifted out of the tub.

With a shriek, Priya announced, "Bear. I'll call you Bear. Only a bear would find itself stuck in a garbage dumpster." And Bear he had remained. A constant companion when she wasn't at work. Over the following weeks, the two had bonded and, when Priya wasn't at work, or out having tea with her only friend, Samantha, the two were inseparable. She let out a deep sigh as the memories flittered around her mind. Sammy rolled her eyes as Priya spoke in the dog's defense, "And he's strong. So, Bear suits him."

"Humph!" Samantha took another sip of her mutilated tea and reached for a scone, copying Priya's actions of opening it, lathering it with butter and jam before enjoying the first bite. "You don't know anything about this dude who's hired you. What was his name?"

"Lord Weatherstone," Priya replied, taking another bite. "But it's his manservant, Horace, who I will have direct dealings with."

"Sounds off, if you ask me."

"They've already deposited a big sum into my bank account," Priya pointed out in their defense. "They've paid me half a year in advance, and I have a month to decide if I want to stay. If I choose to leave within the month, I still get to keep the advance. Sounds more than fair, if you ask me."

The two ladies sat in silence, nibbling on the scones and drinking tea. Samantha broke the silence. "I looked up the location on Google Maps," she said. "Chilcoot Pass is still a hiking trail through the mountains. And White Pass isn't much better. Between avalanches and frigid sub-zero temperatures, this is no place for you and Bear. Do you know how many people died on the trek during the Gold Rush?" She didn't wait for an answer. "Thousands. Besides. How do you expect to drive up into the Boundary Range mountains? Your little VW Golf is no match for the terrain."

"I can drive to Haines Junction," Priya explained. "I've done some research and Horace has provided me with detailed directions to Castle Mutasim. Most of the route, once I'm in Yukon, will be on the Alaskan Highway. There are mountain roads off the highway. I just have to find the right one to lead me to the castle. And it's not as high up into the mountains as Chilcoot Pass. Or White Pass either."

"Still cold up there," Samantha pointed out. "And, in the short summer months, extremely buggy. Take lots of deet."

"Yes, Mom," Priya laughingly responded with a slight shake of her head. She downed the last of her scone and sipped the remaining tepid tea. Glancing at her watch, she announced, "I have to go. Staff meeting."

"Still?" Samantha quirked an eyebrow. "You're leaving in a few days. How can you possibly be required to attend another meeting?"

"I have to hand in my report, sign some papers." Priya shrugged. "All to make the separation official, I guess." She reached across the table to grasp Samantha's hand. "Sammy. We can write, you know."

"There's probably no internet connection where you're going," Samantha pointed out.

"We could use the old-fashioned way of communicating," Priya gave a sheepish grin, giving her friend's hand a warm squeeze. "Snail mail. You know, cursive writing, paper, envelope, address, stamp, mailbox. That kind of thing."

Samantha playfully slapped away Priya's hand. "I know what you mean." The ladies stood and wrapped each other in a warm embrace. "I'll miss you."

"Me, too," Priya agreed, sniffling as tears threatened to mar her cheeks. "Me, too," she repeated. Reaching into her bag, Priya started as Samantha gave a dismissive wave.

"My treat," Samantha claimed. She reached into her own bag and retrieved a wrapped parcel. "For you." She handed it to Priya. "To remember me by."

"Oh, Sammy," Priya sniffled. "You didn't have to. You know I'll remember you and always cherish our friendship."

Samantha pushed the parcel into her friend's hands. "Open it."

Priya took the parcel and, setting her bag on the chair she had vacated, carefully unwrapped the paper. It was a book. Of course. What other treasure could possibly mean as much to her as a book? She gasped. "Cervantes *Don Quixote*! Wow! You knew it's one of my favorites." She ran her hand gingerly over the fabric cover. It was obviously old. The condition was immaculate.

"Look inside," Sammy prodded.

Priya obliged and read, "Best friends forever: Sammy and Priya." With a sniffle, she flipped the page and gasped. "1605. First edition. It's in such good condition. Sammy. I can't accept this. It's too much. It must have cost you a fortune!"

"Only twenty grand in U.S dollars," Sammy shrugged. "You know I come from money."

Taking a deep gulp, Priya closed the book and handed it back to her friend. Or, at least, she tried to. "Still, Sammy. It's too much. I can't accept. I'm flattered by the gesture, though."

Sammy pushed it back toward her friend. "Yes, you can accept it. And you will. I insist. You're the best friend I've ever had." She sniffled. "I don't know what I'll do with you way up north." More sniffles.

"But it's in pristine condition!" Priya exclaimed. "It looks brand new. Instead of over four hundred years old."

"Look at the back," her friend insisted, turning the book over and opening the back cover. "See how it's been repaired."

"Expertly, I'd say. I wouldn't have noticed if you hadn't pointed it out." She studied the care given to repairing the back cover. To making the book whole again. "It's remarkable. I love it. But I can't accept it, Sammy. It's too much."

"It's not too much. It's the perfect gift for the best friend who loves books, and Don Quixote I must add, almost more than anything else." Priya couldn't resist a chuckle. Sammy joined in as she nudged the book closer to her friend.

With a reluctant nod, Priya accepted the book, wrapping it back in the paper it came in and tucking it into her bag. "Thank you, Sammy. I'll treasure it always."

The two hugged. Sniffled. Hugged some more. Then Sammy pushed away and said, "Off you go to your meeting. And you keep yourself, and your mutt, safe."

"In other words, don't do anything you wouldn't do."

"Exactly."

CHAPTER THREE

Present

"It's okay, Priya," a calming voice reached deep into her subconscious. "I'm here. I'm going to help you."

The black hole in which she swirled evaporated slightly. As the darkness dissipated, the pain returned. And the cold. She couldn't remember ever being this cold. A whimper tickled her ear bringing her closer to the surface of consciousness. "Bear?" Had she spoken. Was it her voice she heard? All crackled and incoherent? She was rewarded with another whimper and a wet nose against her bare hand, the one screaming with pain. And cold.

"Bear?" she forced herself to speak to the only one close by. "Are you okay, Bear?" She couldn't say anything else. Her voice was brittle dry and the words she emitted were garbled.

"He's okay, Priya." The voice again. Closer. "And so are you. You called and I came. Now let's get you out of here and someplace warm." The voice droned on. Soothing. Comforting. Warm.

"Amell?" she whispered his name.

"Yes, Priya. I am here."

CHAPTER FOUR

She barely remembered the sensation of her seatbelt being unfastened and her stiff limbs manoeuvred from their frozen positions before she was lifted from the car. She barely remembered being placed on a soft rug of a sleigh, Bear positioned next to her so they could share warmth, rugs covering them both. She barely remembered the cacophony of barking dogs, or Amell's voice issuing orders to others, instructing them to unload the car and leave it.

Her things. Her possessions. What happened to all she packed to bring to her new home, her new job? Had it been left buried with the car? Somewhere down an icy cliff? Off the road in the middle of nowhere?

"Where am I?" she spoke before her eyes opened. She felt warm. Cocooned. Safe. Bear whimpered a response. "Bear? Where are you?" A wet muzzle, cold, touched the bare skin of her hand, sending shards of pain up her arms.

"You are at Castle Mutasim, Priya." A woman's voice. Unfamiliar. But soft. Warm. Comforting.

She wrenched open one eye. Then the other. Barely. Squinting at the light.

"Who are you?"

"Katarina. Please just call me Kat."

"Kat." She struggled to open her eyes further, fighting the piercing pain caused by the light. "What time is it? How long have I been here? My car? My things?"

"The men took care of bringing your possessions from the car." The woman patted Priya's arm gently. "Everything is stacked in the adjacent room. As for the car? It may be buried by now. Or at the bottom of the chasm. You are lucky to be alive. You and your dog. Bear, you called him."

Bear whimpered at the sound of his name. "Is he alright?" she asked, concern evident in the tone of her voice. "Is Bear okay?"

"A few bruises that'll heal. Same with you," Kat replied. "The two of you managed to keep each other warm."

Priya's eyes were fully open. She bit back a gasp when she saw the woman seated next to her. If it's what she was. Grizzled facial features which appeared more feline than human; long hair, tangled and sweeping around her head in the most unruly fashion. And the hands. The one closest to Priya, the one patting Priya's arm. It was more claw than hand with sharp nails protruding from the base of what on an animal would be called a paw. "Kat," she felt a sharp intake of breath. "What are you?" She couldn't help herself. She had to know.

Kat's face brightened into what might be interpreted as a smile. It was difficult to tell. "I am an experiment in genetic manipulation that went quite wrong," she explained simply. "But I'm more than half human, so that should count for something even if I don't appear human."

"And your kind," Priya admitted. "What is this place? Is this really Castle Mutasim? The name means refuge, doesn't it?"

Kat nodded her head. "And that's exactly what it is. A refuge. For people-if you care to call us human-like me. Hidden in an isolated part of the world so, no one can take us away. No one can use us for experiments. It's our safe place."

"So, everyone here is," she struggled for the right word and finally settled on, "different, like you."

"Everyone is different," Kat agreed. "Even those who believe they're human to the core. They are all different from one another."

Now it was Priya's turn to attempt a smile. "True enough. But why am I here? I'm not different in the same way as you and the others at Castle Mutasim. Or am I?"

"You'll have to ask Amell, Priya." The woman patted Priya's arm again. "Now, perhaps you should try to sleep. You and Bear here will feel much better after a good night's sleep, cuddled together and staying warm. In the morning, I'll fix you a nice hot bath to ease the aching muscles and bruises. But, right now, what you need most is sleep."

Priya didn't have the energy to argue. She had more questions, but they'd have to wait. Her eyes were closing on their own accord, and she didn't have the willpower to fight back. With Bear snuggled close to her side, Priya slipped into a deep, dreamless sleep.

CHAPTER FIVE

It was dark when Priya woke again. There was a glow coming from what must be a hearth. A few crackles suggested a fire gently burning, keeping her and Bear warm and comfy. An outline of a shadow hovered between her and the glowing hearth.

"You're awake." It was neither a statement nor a question. The voice was soothing. Comforting. The same reassuring voice she remembered from the crash site. The same voice from further back. She was sure she knew the voice. But how? When? Where?

"Amell?" she asked in little more than a whisper. Why did the name keep surfacing to the forefront of her memory? Why did she know this name? She couldn't recall anyone in her past named Amell. Or did she?

"Yes," came the calm answer. "They did a good job erasing your memory. But they couldn't erase a love as deep as ours."

"You're my brother. Amell." Priya pushed herself partway into a sitting position. Felt a wave of dizziness. Stopped. The weight at her feet stirred and whimpered. "Bear." She reached over, sinking the fingers of one hand into his thick fir. He was good at offering comfort. Reassurance.

"He's a good dog," came the reply. And then more. "And, yes, I am your brother, Amell."

"You disappeared," she claimed, the memories buried for so long reaching for the surface. Fragments. Disjointed. Amell reading to her as they snuggled together on the couch. Amell teaching her to catch. Amell wiping away the tears when she scraped a knee, or a schoolmate teased her relentlessly. How could she have forgotten the bond? The love? "So long ago. What happened?"

"You were only a child," he admitted. "They didn't want you to understand. They didn't want you to miss me. So, they erased your memory. Or at least they tried to."

"It must have worked," Priya surmised. "At least, until a few days ago I didn't even know the name Amell, let alone someone who bore the name." She sat up further. Waited for the room to settle. When it did, she swung her legs over the side of the bed, sitting fully upright. "Amell. Power of an eagle. You always were strong. Brave. You were my world. And then you were gone."

"And then I was gone," he echoed her sentiments. "I have missed you, Priya. Beautiful. Beloved. My Priya. My little sister." He let out a deep sigh. "I followed you. From a distance. I watched you grow up. Become the woman you are today. I am so proud of you, Priya."

"Why didn't you reach out before?" she asked, sniffling slightly at Amell's sentimental comments. "Why this ruse to get me up here? And why such an isolated setting? And who owns this place? Are you Lord Weatherstone? And who's Horace?"

Amell let out the soft, heartfelt chuckle she remembered so well. "So many questions, little Priya. You were always one full of questions." He paused. "First. I own this place. There is no Lord Weatherstone. Nor is there a Horace. All names created to lure you here. To bring you to a safe place."

"But how? And why did you leave us?" The room was starting to brighten; daylight creeped through the cracks between the drapes. A streak of light cast an eery glow across the floor, landing like a stage light on Amell's left face. She gasped softly. Squinted. Studied his profile intensely. The light accentuated the long, golden tresses of a lion's mane, the deep creases of a wizened face, part lion, part human. The skin tone was bronzed, the eyes large, fully dark unlike the human eye. And the mouth. Her eyes were drawn to the lips, thick and tough, barely opening as Amell spoke.

"I didn't look like this when I left." He understood her shock. Sensed it. Felt it deep within his core. "I was only a teenager in human years, still learning how to primp myself daily in front of a mirror. I managed to hide most of the changes, shaving several times a day, applying makeup, wearing bulky clothing. By the time I was sixteen, it was overwhelming. I was more lion than human. I heard our parents talking one night. It was late. You were long asleep. They were afraid I would give into my wild genes and become a danger to them. And to you.

"They made arrangements for me to be removed the next day, while you were at school. They had contacted the authorities; the lab which produced me. Made the necessary arrangements. I had to leave. Who knows what horrible experiments they'd subject me to? All in the name of science. I have since learned, from others who now live here in our only refuge that it was, at best, a horrible experience. And there are thousands more. Millions, perhaps. Mutated genetic creations. All being used and abused for testing. For science. For them."

"But how did you survive? How did you manage to afford this place?"

"I was clever, Priya." He maintained a patient tone, even though it was strained. It was obvious to Priya he suffered inwardly as he unveiled his past. "I was always good with numbers. Good in math. I had some money saved, stashed away from odd jobs done here and there. It was enough to tide me over until I could make it work for me. I changed my name, took up residence in a tiny apartment above a Chinese grocer in Vancouver's Chinatown. I laid low, making sure there was no way anyone could track me."

"They must have inserted implants in you," Priya pointed out. "So, you couldn't escape. Disappear."

She watched as the mangy head nodded with slow reverence. "They did. I didn't know at first. I thought I was clever, leaving behind all my high-tech stuff: computers, phones, etc. They found me anyway. I noticed them snooping around, asking questions. Once again, I gathered my meagre possessions and dwindling finances and made a hasty exit. Headed for the mountains. I stumbled on another mutated creature, Danny, and he was able to assist me in discovering and removing the tracking device. We dumped it in the Fraser River and made a hasty exit deeper into the mountains. I lived off the land for a year. Danny and I parted ways the following spring. I made tracks north and ended up in Prince George. Once again, I moved into a nondescript apartment in the poorer section of town. Did odd jobs to pay the rent and to eat. I always did have a voracious appetite."

Priya broke the tension with a slight chuckle. "I remember, now. You used to clean up my plate and anyone else's after you finished yours. Even the family dog had to finish his meal quickly or be left without."

Amell snorted. "I wasn't that bad, was I?"

"Perhaps not. Childhood memories, especially those erased and slowly creeping back, can be inflated."

"To say the least." The two shared a gentle laugh. "Somehow I landed a gig as a bouncer at a night club. Made some good tips. Met some of the wrong people. But managed to start seriously making money. And finding new ways to make my money grow. One night, I got wind of a big bust. Just as the police were raiding the front of the establishment, I broke into the club's safe and packed up the stash of bills and gold bars. It was a lot. No human could carry as much as I did. Nor could a human make the escape I did."

"The mobsters must have been after you when they realized you had their loot."

Amell shook his head. "Funny thing was, they didn't know it was me. They believed the cops took it in the raid and some dirty cop pocketed the lot. Either way, I decided it was time to move on. I made some wise investments, which doubled within a few months. Returned south and made my way to one of the Gulf

Islands after another, discovering a huge population of once-upon-a-time hippies who continue to live off the grid. Each group welcomed me without question and most likely forgot about me as soon as I disappeared again. Tired of trying to make myself presentable in the human form, I finally returned to Vancouver Island where I discovered this property, deep in the forests, off the grid. It was up for sale. Believe it or not, someone wanted to sell this land which really should be a protected space. Doesn't matter. It was a refuge for me, a place where I could just be me: part human, part lion. Others like me found my refuge and together we built the fortress. We work hard to protect it and it's so out of the way and unknown to the outside world that we can literally do what we want without complications from the law. I keep an office in Comox to maintain a legal address from which I continue to make investments."

"Money laundering."

"In a sense, yes. But I do have morals, Priya. I invest wisely and legally."

"So, why bring me here? Why now? And why the ruse of cataloguing and preserving a vast collection of books and artifacts?"

"That is your expertise, is it not?" he challenged gently. "I wasn't sure you'd come if I told you who I was."

"Fair enough," Priya agreed with a slight nod of the head. "You do have a collection for me to take care of?"

"Of course," Amell exclaimed, his chest puffing out demonstrating a sense of pride. "Better than anything you cared for in the archives in Victoria. As well as making money, I enjoy the frivolous nature of spending it. Mostly on things of quality and lasting pleasure: books, art and, you'd be surprised, musical instruments."

"Really?"

"Really. More later. I hear Kat's gentle footsteps. She'll be here in a minute, probably scolding me for keeping you up. After you've had time to get dressed and eat some breakfast, I'll give you the grand tour. Kat will know where to find me."

He stood to leave, slipping out through a cavity in the wall, a secret door behind the fireplace. Kat knocked and entered. She sniffed her feline nose intently. Knowingly. "He was here, wasn't he?"

Priya merely shrugged her shoulders.

CHAPTER SIX

While Priya sipped the soothing mug of tea Kat placed on her side table, she listened to the steady sound of running water in the adjoining bathroom. The tea soaked through every pore in her body, giving her a small illusion of normalcy. She never had developed a liking for coffee, tea being her go-to warm drink. How did they know? She pondered and shrugged aside the question. It appeared there was a lot others knew about her. It was unnerving. Seeking solace, she reached across her bed to Bear and gently ran her fingers across the top of his head and along the length of his back.

"Still aching buddy?" she asked. Her touch was gentle, but she noticed his body wince and she heard the subdued whimper as her hand made contact in certain locations. "Bruised there, huh?" Tail thump. Eyes focused on the caregiver. "We'll have to see about your aches, too, won't we?"

"Bath's ready," Kat announced, having slipped back into the room without a sound. "I'll take Bear down to the kitchen and outside. Amell will have some tonic to help him heal. He has a tender, healing touch."

"He always did," Priya agreed, her hand continuing to stroke Bear. *Where did that little snippet of memory come from?* she asked herself and immediately envisioned a childhood blip of running in the backyard. Falling. Scraping her knees. Crying for help. Amell to the rescue. A hand over the wound. The blood disappearing. The pain evaporating.

Back to the present. "What do you say, Bear?" She glanced lovingly at her dog. "Will you be able to get up and make the trek downstairs for food, water and a visit outside?" A slight thump of the tail. "Will you allow Amell to heal you?" Another thump.

"He's already started," Kat explained. "Last night when you arrived. Bear was pretty beat up. Bruised. Bloody. He had shards of glass from the windshield embedded all along his back and even in his paws. One cut at a time, Amell healed both you and your dog. All while you slept. A good bath will erase the rest of your aches, my dear. And by the time you're ready to come down for some breakfast, Bear will be bounding around like his old self."

"Did you hear, Bear?" She gave him a gentle scratch behind the ear. His favorite scratch spot. Tail thump.

"I've unpacked your clothes and laid out some for the day," Kat chattered on. "You'll need to dress warmer up here than you're used to in the south. If you don't like what I selected, I'll leave it to you to make the change." She patted her thigh with the paw-like hands and called to Bear, "Come along, Bear. Amell and pain relief await."

Bear whimpered as he struggled to lever himself onto all four paws. Jumping cautiously off the bed, he did a few stretches before padding along after Kat. At the door, he glanced back at Priya, who waved him off with a fond, "Off you go, Bear. I'll be down soon." The two were out the door, leaving Priya alone.

She remained seated on the bed, replaying the past few hours in her head as she allowed her eyes to roam around the room, taking in the surroundings which were clearer now with the daylight streaming in through the cracks in the drapes. It was bright. She didn't need overhead lights. She had good night vision, always had. The streak of outdoor light and the bathroom light only served as a spotlight to highlight certain areas of the room.

It was a big room. Spacious. Although the fire in the stone hearth was slowly dying out, the room maintained a comforting warmth. Bookcases lined the walls on either side of the hearth. All full of books. She'd have to peruse the collection later. Perhaps it was part of her assignment. All to be catalogued. The mantel over the stone hearth was polished to a fine shine and sported a lovely, ornate clock which was ticking with soothing accuracy. She hadn't noticed the tick-tocks during the night. It was a subtle nuance of sound which seemed to settle the oratorial environment of the space.

A large window, draped, dominated the far confines. A spinet desk positioned centrally, presumably to allow the person seated at the desk to look out into the world while working. The wall opposite the hearth, with the bed, was lined with another bookcase, a large dresser, a gold framed, floor-length mirror, and a door which presumably opened into a closet. She'd explore it later.

Of immediate interest was the door leading to the bathroom and the soothing comfort of a bath which awaited.

She pushed herself off the bed and made her way to the inviting comfort of the waiting bath. Pushing the door inward, Priya stepped into the misty warmth. A light shone overhead, flickering a haze which engulfed her as she stepped into the bathroom and shut the door behind her. The room was larger than the living room in the apartment she'd left behind. The mosaic tiled floors felt cool, but everything else was steaming with a soothing heat.

The vanity included a lengthy countertop to lay out her personal toiletries, which, it appeared, Kat had already unpacked and set out for her. The sink was a deep blue, shell-shaped and lacking the standard enameled surfacing of an industrially produced sink. It appeared hand crafted, possibly pottery, kiln-fired and glazed. The faucets were equally unique, not the standard issue from the neighborhood hardware store. A gold-gilded mirror, thick with mist, hung over the vanity, flashing a vision in Priya's mind of Snow White's wicked stepmother and her chanting, "Mirror, mirror, on the wall." She almost mouthed the words out loud, but thought better of it. Too much was suggesting magic and the mayhem resulting from magic. She didn't want to tempt fate.

The bathtub was immense. Sitting on claw feet, it lured her forward with a promise of a good, long soak. And there were bubbles. A bubble bath. She was a sucker for bubble baths. She quickly removed her attire, allowing the clothes to remain where they fell. Stepping into the bath, she let out a satisfied moan and slipped deep into the foaming surface, sliding down into the comfort beneath.

"Oh!" she let out another groan of pleasure as the warmth soaked into every pore and every aching muscle and joint.

As she soaked and washed away the grime of the previous day, memories flashed through her mind: memories of childhood romps with her older brother, Amell; memories of the horrid drive up the mountainside in a blizzard, and the traumatic tumble off the road's edge.

Amell. Always strong, assured, confident. Protective, too. He watched out for Priya as a child. Carefully coaxed her to take her first steps, throw and catch her first ball. It was the little things that flooded her brain. Evenings spent curled up next to Amell as he patiently read one picture book after another until she fell asleep. Later, he was equally patient as she stumbled over the words, learning to sound them out, reading one word at a time. These were memories one would expect to include parents. They didn't. These memories included Amell. It was later, after his sudden disappearance and the erasure of her memories when parental involvement replaced Amell's presence.

She couldn't recall when the changes began. When Amell started to sprout mounds of facial hair. When he spent hours, multiple times a day, holed up in the family washroom, shaving it all off.

And then he was gone. She cried for days, until the memories ceased to exist, and the tears dried up.

There were blank spots in this resurrected memory bank, but the important parts were there, most specifically Amell's love for Priya. His younger sister.

Is he really who he says he is? He claims to have been genetically engineered in a lab, as are others living here.

She shook her head to clear the cobwebs of confusion. Slipping deeper into the bubbles, her mind morphed around the events of the past couple of days.

After parting company with Samantha, she had returned to the archives. There was a scheduled staff meeting planned for the afternoon, so she made her way to the large conference meeting room. Walking through the door, she was decorated with confetti, as everyone cheered and applauded. Balloons and streamers flittered about the room and a table covered with goodies made Priya wish she hadn't eaten so much for lunch. There was even a large slab cake (chocolate, of course) emblazoned with the words: *Wishing you well in the castle!* Most of her colleagues knew about her new job. Up north. In a castle. They all romanticized with her, assuring Priya a fairy tale life awaited her, complete with a charming prince to sweep her off her feet. Priya wasn't so sure. It was merely a job. One she was trained to do. One she loved: working with books and artifacts.

Stuffed with good food and going-away gifts, including a thick hoodie, like the ones sold in the gift shop, sporting the phrase: *Archives Do It* Better, along with the archive logo.

"You'll need warm clothes where you're going," someone joked. She couldn't remember who.

Another person added, "And we didn't want you to forget us when your brain cells froze."

After the going-away party, the last few days seemed to drag as there was little left to do at her old job but pack up the few remaining personal items from her desk. On Friday afternoon, she made the final farewells, some with hugs and promises to stay in touch. The following day, Saturday, car packed and apartment cleaned, she dropped off the keys with the landlord and headed out.

The first part of the journey was uneventful. The hour wait at the ferry terminal was standard procedure, as was the smooth, two-hour crossing to Vancouver. The drive through the lower mainland was shrouded in overcast, dreary, raining weather, so typical of early spring. The clouds became heavier the further north she drove. When she crossed the border into Yukon, the rain had changed into sleet and then snow.

It was a long trek. The first night, she checked into a roadside inn just north of Kamloops. The second night she spent in Prince George, followed by a night in Watson Lake and then Whitehorse. The drive to Haines Junction had been short enough, though the visibility from the thickening accumulation of snow had made it difficult to see mere feet in front of the car. Once she left the highway, the route instructions led her around Kluane National Park, meandering the perimeter of the flat plains, leading toward Mount Logan, Canada's highest mountain. From her research, she knew the mountain loomed ahead, but the weather blocked out all panoramic views, save the fluttering flurries enveloping the vehicle like a thick shroud.

Curled up next to her, Bear whimpered his concerns. She wanted to curl up next to him, but she knew she couldn't stop. They'd be buried alive in mere minutes. Gripping the steering wheel more firmly, she shrieked in frustration, "This is nuts. It's spring, for heaven's sake. Not winter." A voice deep within muttered in response, *Welcome to the far north.*

She didn't know when or how the road started climbing, but the car was struggling. She saw the first turn, just in time, yanking the steering wheel to guide the car around the steep bend, only to have to do it again and again as the road fishtailed up the mountainside, bouncing from one pothole and crater to another as it hugged the road precariously seeking refuge from a steep drop.

Then she missed a turn. It was her last conscious thought, other than her call out to Amell. And she was cold. Oh, so cold.

Amell came to her rescue. She knew he would. How? She didn't know for sure.

Now, here she was, soaking in a warm, soothing bath, safe in a castle far away from her original destination. Certainly, it was nowhere near Mount Logan.

Taking in several deep breath, lathering her body once more, she focussed her thoughts on the here and the now. Reluctantly, she stood up and climbed out of the bath, reaching for the large towel hanging within arm's reach. Dried off, she pulled on the clothes laid out for her, snuggling deep into the warmth, not allowing the chill from leaving the soothing bath to penetrate too deep. She brushed and dried her hair, cleaned her teeth and walked out of the bathroom, content she was ready to face the new day. Her first day in this isolated castle somewhere on Vancouver Island.

CHAPTER SEVEN

Kat was waiting for her. "I'll take you to the dining room. Amell awaits. I'm sure he'll want to give you a tour of the castle later and fill you in on your duties. We all work here. And I know you came intent to pursue a new job in your chosen career. I just hope you are happy at Castle Mutasim. You will find the inhabitants quite different from the people you lived and worked with in the south. On the outside. Deep down, though, they're all kind-hearted and hard-working souls." She opened the door and led Priya into the hall. "There. Already I've said too much. Come along. I'm sure you're famished after yesterday's ordeal."

Without another word, Kat ushered Priya down the hall to a grand staircase, leading to the main floor. A quick turn to the right at the foot of the stairs and along another hall, then Kat slid open pocket doors, opening into a well-lit grand dining area. To say it was huge would be an understatement.

Amell was standing beside a sideboard, plate in hand, stacking it with bacon, eggs, biscuits, and all kinds of fruit. Priya stifled a chuckle, remembering how she used to tease her older brother and his voracious appetite.

He seemed to sense her amusement. "No teasing," he spoke calmly as he continued to pile his plate high. "There's still lots for you. Though I suspect you still eat like a bird." Receiving no response, he moved away from the sideboard, carrying his plate to the head of the long, finely polished wood table. It was probably oak; Priya couldn't be sure as she wasn't an expert on different woods.

Candelabra graced the table from one end to the other, unlit, saved for darkened days and evening's ambiance. A large, central chandelier hung over the table, providing more than enough light.

The warmth permeated from a roaring fire in the stone-studded fireplace, situated between rows of French doors, presumably leading outside. Sunlight filtered through the windows, but the glitter was blinding as it reflected off the billions of snow crystals piled high and for as far as the eye could see. The sight of snow made her shudder at the memory of the previous day's events: the blinding climb up steep mountain roads, the fast descent over the side of a cliff, the intense cold.

Kat appeared at Priya's side and draped an arm across her shoulders. The warmth of her slight embrace was enough to still the shivers which threatened just beneath the surface. Taking a deep breath, she focussed on assessing the contents of the room more thoroughly, if, for no other reason than to block the chilling memories.

The table was set for at least a dozen, as if others were expected. As Priya remained rooted on the precipice of the entryway, she was nudged aside rather abruptly.

"Oh. Sorry, Miss," a crackly voice offered an apology. "But I must get some food before Amell devours it all. He does that sometimes, you know."

The sudden chatter was all Priya needed to break her stance. She laughed heartily. "Oh, how well I know Amell's appetite."

"Roderick," Amell bellowed as he forked some bacon and eggs, preparing to shovel it into his mouth. "Show some manners and introduce yourself to my sister."

"Ah. Miss Priya," Roderick bowed deeply, taking Priya's hand in his furry paws. "Welcome to Castle Mutasim. We've heard so much about you. Amell talks of no one else." As he glanced up, he gave what might have been interpreted as a smile, but it was hard to tell. His head was the shape of a fox, pointed snout, dark, steely eyes and a deep red tongue which flickered in and out of his mouth as he talked.

Priya, ever the diplomat, covered her curiosity with ease and rewarded the creature known as Roderick with a warm smile.

"Thank you, Roderick. And just call me Priya. We all know I'm a Miss." Coyly stealing a glance at her brother, she added teasingly, "At least, I believe we all do."

Amell merely grunted and turned his attention to the plate full of food sitting before him. Roderick scurried off to get his own grub. He was fast. Wiley and quick like a fox. He was seated with his plateful (not as substantially full as Amell's) in a blink of an eye. Priya heard more footsteps approaching and decided it was time to make her move before she was barrelled over by others. Besides, her stomach was telling her she was hungry.

Priya piled a plate higher than she normally would have done. *Bear will come and help me finish what I can't eat,* she reasoned in her mind. In reality, she was convinced she could eat all the bacon, eggs, two biscuits, a muffin and a bowl of fruit, and still want for more. This was so unlike her. *What's happening to me?* She pondered. More questions. So few answers. *I don't usually eat this much for breakfast. Or ever, for that matter.*

She claimed the empty seat next to Amell, intent on talking while she ate. She didn't have a chance to speak. Voices crowded into the room, dishes clanged, chairs pulled back. All the residents of the castle, it appeared, were sharing breakfast together in the grand dining room. Even Bear.

"Bear?" she almost shrieked, dropping her fork which clattered on the plate. "Is that you?" A dog-like figure carried a platter piled high with bacon, just bacon. He walked on his hind legs like a human, but his tail and mouth, complete with the long red tongue swishing in and out of his mouth, suggested he was more dog than human. As he should be. "Bear?" she gasped.

"Yes, Priya," the creature replied. "It is I. The one you call Bear. Perhaps you could come up with another name. Like Gawain. Or Wayne, for short."

His suggestion was met with guffaws all around the table. "He fashions himself after the great Sir Gawain," Roderick paused from his eating long enough to explain, pointing a fork at Bear.

"Knight in shining armor. Rescuer of damsels in distress and all that."

Priya glanced from one face to another, then back at Bear. "What does he mean?"

"I've always been as you see me now, Priya," Bear explained. "You rescued me as a mutt. Or what you perceived as a mutt. For that I am grateful. But that was the intent. So I could be with you always and protect you."

"Protect me?" she gasped. "From what? From whom?"

"From the same evil powers that created all of us," Roderick explained quickly, then shoved bacon into his mouth, astutely dropping his eyes out of Amell's steely glare.

Priya turned to Amell. "What does he mean?" she asked. "Why did I need protection?"

"You're one of us, Priya." Amell let out a deep sigh. "I wasn't sure how to protect you. How to tell you. Now Roderick's told you."

"But I showed no symptoms," she argued. "Nothing visual. Nothing to suggest I'm different."

"But you are different," Amell explained. "And because your differences aren't visual, at least most of the time, you're more valuable to them than the rest of us."

"I don't understand." She dropped her cutlery on the plate with a clatter, the hunger which had besieged her earlier dissipating rapidly. Pushing her chair back, she stood up. Glaring first at Amell, then at Bear, she proclaimed, "I loved and trusted both of you. And you both betrayed me. How could you?"

"Priya," Amell reached out to take her hand, but she had pulled it away too fast, anticipating his actions. She ran from the room and made a beeline in the direction she hoped would lead to the grand staircase, hoping she'd find her way back to the rooms she'd been assigned.

She didn't. She must have made a wrong turn in her haste to escape what she didn't want to hear. Pausing to catch her breath, and to listen, she was reassured no one was following. Doors lined the hall on either side; one stood slightly ajar. The pocket doors, thick wooden panels, were open just enough for her to slip through. Which she did. Once through the precipice, she glanced around, her eyes taking in the glassed-in surroundings, the reams of plants of all different shapes and sizes. Warmth soaked through her skin; she breathed in the thick, moist air.

She closed her eyes briefly to savor the moment. Opening them, her eyes nearly popped at the sight right before her.

"Oh my!" she exclaimed, taking one tentative step forward, followed by another. "Mom's piano. How did it get here?"

CHAPTER EIGHT

"Roderick!" Amell boomed. "When will you learn to keep quiet?"

"Never," someone at the far end of the table muttered, loud enough for those around him to share a chuckle.

"Wiley and sly as a fox," another voice added to the melee. "At least part of him is. The other part is uncontrollable gossip."

"Enough!" Amell boomed.

"Shall I follow her?" Bear asked, taking a repast from devouring the platter of bacon. He licked his chops and awaited an answer. "She has a right to know, Amell. You know that as well as I do. As well as the rest of us. She should have been told years ago. Brought here long before the trouble fell on her doorstep."

Amell sat back down, placing his elbows on the table and dropping his chin into the palms of what might be hands or paws, or both. "No, Wayne," he honored Bear with the name Priya's beloved pet had requested. "I shall go. But first you must fill us all in. What transpired to make your urgent request a month ago?"

"They came to her apartment," Bear, or more accurately, Wayne, began. Finally allowed the privilege of being able to talk like a human instead of masquerading as a mongrel dog, he bristled with a modicum of pride.

"Who?"

"Them," Wayne continued bluntly. "The ones who created us. Or at least their bouncers, or whatever you want to call them."

"The security detail," Amell suggested. He nodded. "Continue."

"Priya was at work," he went on. "They picked the locks and slipped inside. I don't think they knew about me. I put on my best doggy act, barking up a storm until the police arrived to survey the situation. I guess one of the neighbors complained about my incessant barking. I had them cornered, but when the sirens approached, they just vanished."

"Nothing just vanishes," Roderick snorted in disbelief.

"Somehow they cloaked themselves, so they were invisible," Wayne snapped in defense. "The door opened again, then closed. They were invisible and they slipped out. I ceased barking, merely growling as I sniffed around. A barking dog complaint was filed and Priya was served a fine. She scolded me."

"I gather that wasn't the end of it," Amell pressed on.

"No." Wayne admitted. "They returned. This time armed with something to deactivate me."

"You can't deactivate a living creature," Roderick snorted again in disbelief.

"They rendered me unconscious, then. Is that better?" He stole an angry glare at Roderick seated opposite him.

"Enough children!" Amell snapped, a growl rumbling from deep within his chest. "We don't have time for childish quibbles. Continue, Wayne."

"When I came to, I was in Priya's home, but something seemed off." Wayne paused long enough to sneak another strip of bacon. Once he swallowed, he continued. "Sorry. Priya fed me well enough, but it was all that dry doggy kibble. Nothing nourishing like this."

"Carry on," Amell urged.

Wayne cleared his throat. "I recalled the entrance of the goons and decided to sniff out the place. I found cameras and recorders hidden in every room and every corner. They were spying on Priya. Possibly me as well. Somehow, I managed to maintain my full dogginess. Though I can't be sure what happened while I was out cold. I decided to leave the devices in place, as I didn't want to incur concern on their part and have them return."

"How do you know you weren't compromised?" Roderick asked.

"I didn't," Wayne admitted. "So, I took down the device in the room where I woke and downloaded the filming onto Priya's laptop. Which was also compromised, I might add, but I managed to block that. Anyway," he cleared his throat again. "I studied the images captured in the camera. It appears they implanted me with a tracking device. In my neck, if you can believe it. Of all the places. Luckily, in my semi-human form, and working in front of the bathroom mirror (the one room, out of decency, they hadn't wired with a camera), I was able to extract it. Made a bloody mess, which Priya scolded me about later. I flushed the device down the toilet and hoped they had a good visual of our plumbing as it descended into the bowels of the city sewage system."

The last comment earned a few guffaws from around the table.

"But it must have alerted them," Roderick suggested.

"Perhaps," Wayne agreed. "I guess not enough for them to return. I thought it best to reach out and make the situation known to you. To see if it would be prudent to bring Priya here. For her safety."

"Good thoughts, Wayne. Good job done." Amell started to stand, then paused. "Sorry it took us so long to rescue you and Priya. We hadn't meant the accident to be so serious. But the weather was unexpected."

"We're here, now, Amell," Wayne assured the others. "It's all that matters. Now, are you off to speak to Priya? Or should I?"

"I'll go," Amell insisted, standing up to his full height. "One last question. Did you remove her implant?"

"Yes," Wayne admitted. "It wasn't easy. She's not a deep sleeper. I removed it while she slept in that dreadful dump we stayed in while passing through Prince George. Don't know why she couldn't find a better hotel enroute." He shuddered noticeably.

Amell nodded. "We can only hope that there are no more implants. In either of you." His voice echoed a note of concern. "We can't risk them finding us here." Clearing his throat, he turned to leave. "I shall seek her out. In the meantime, the rest of you have things to attend to. We must make sure all the tracking devices attached to Priya and her belongings have been deactivated and discarded. We shall reconvene at lunch."

He briskly marched out of the dining room in search of his sister. He knew where to look. The strains of a Gershwin masterpiece were filling every cavity in the castle. He may not have been living at home when his sister excelled as a musician, but he had managed to sneak around when others were oblivious to his presence. To listen. To observe. He knew Priya's favorite compositions and her pristine talent as well as if he had been at home while her musicianship matured. She had found her piano. Her music. Her solace.

CHAPTER NINE

She only stood on the precipice of the room for a few minutes, before entering with reverence. Her eyes no longer took in the menagerie of plants and the clear glass windows which allowed a bright array of sunlight to trickle through. She only had eyes for the piano. Her mother's treasured possession. A late nineteenth-century Heinzman, baby grand, slightly longer in length than the traditional baby grand. With ivory keys and highly satin-glossed walnut exterior, complete with elaborately carved trim and legs, the piano was a work of art in itself. One of a kind. And the soft, poignant sound it created was like music from the hemispheres, a tribute to the spruce wood soundboard which backed the well stretched, quality strings. Everything about the piano was pure beauty.

After her parents died in a tragic car accident, about ten years ago, Priya had planned to sell most of their belongings, including the house where she grew up. The piano would go, too, since Priya didn't have space large enough for the piano. She had contemplated moving into her childhood home, but the taxes alone, not to mention the services and insurance, was more than her meagre salary could manage. There wasn't any money in the inheritance, only property. And, sadly, there was a considerable mortgage remaining on the house. The only alternative was to sell and settle her parents' debts. Living in an apartment for the short term was the only option. She had begun the process of packing things, selling items, moving what she could into her apartment. But fate had another idea in store. While unpacking her latest collection of boxes littering her tiny apartment space, a phone call alerted Priya to the tragedy which had befallen the house. Engulfed in flames, it was reduced to rubble before Priya could respond to the notification. Anything which hadn't already been packed and moved to the apartment, including the piano, was gone.

Fire investigators had deemed the incident as arson. Since there was a large insurance policy on the house and possessions, and the outstanding mortgage was fully insured, the authorities diverted their attention to Priya as the arsonist. Evidence alighted to prove her innocence, but the scar of the tragedy and the implicated accusations remained. The only bright side to the tragedy was the release from a crippling debt her parents had passed on.

So, if everything perished in the fire, how did the piano get here? It was the same piano. She was sure of it. Her mother's piano was a one-of-the-kind creation. Heintzman didn't duplicate his masterpieces. And this was one of his originals.

All questions vanished as she ran her hand gingerly, lovingly along the smoothly polished surface. She made her way around the piano, finally settling in, taking a seat and allowing her fingers to touch the keys. After running through a few scales, it felt like she was home. Really and truly home. Without thinking, she launched into her signature piece, an all-time favorite, Gershwin's *Rhapsody in Blue*.

Composed and first performed in 1924, this composition by George Gershwin was intended for solo piano and jazz band. A jazz piece, so typical of the roaring twenties, it mirrored the classical form of the concerto. Although written as a piano concerto, the piece was often performed on solo piano, as was Priya's preference. She had enjoyed the piece in her younger years, resorting to it whenever she needed to restore some modicum of balance in her life. Like now.

As she pounded out the large chord progressions and eased into the ragtime rhythm, she felt her body relax. The insecurities and uncertainties of the past few days melted way. She worked through the entire composition; the piece long committed to memory. The years spent away from a piano had not dimmed her recollection. There had been many times when she had resorted to singing various parts of the work. The immediate world around her melted away; all that remained was her, the piano and the music. As it should be.

With the final chord still echoing through the conservatory space, Priya was startled out of her reverie by enthusiastic applause. She glanced at the source and almost broke into a smile seeing Amell standing off to one side. Almost. Then the unanswered questions crashed inside her skull, along with the feeling of betrayal. Amell had betrayed her years ago by disappearing. Amell betrayed her again by planting Bear in her home as a spy or protector, she didn't know which. Amell betrayed her by bringing her here. Wherever here was.

Amell broke the awkward silence. "You always had a musical talent. Must be the dolphin in you. Or the elephant. Or both."

Priya bolted from the piano bench and walked around to lean against its side. Arms crossed; she faced her brother with defiance. "The what?" she demanded. "I'm human, Amell. All of me. I'm not a mutant like you and the others."

Stunned, Amell stepped back as if slapped. Priya as the child he once knew had never before spoken to him with such vengeance. With such mean language. She almost, not quite, but almost sounded like a schoolyard bully. Mutant indeed. Pulling himself together, he spoke as calmly as his shattered ego would allow. "I am not a mutant, Priya. And you know it. I was created in a lab. A blending of human and various animal genes. As were the others here. As were you."

"I was not created in a lab!" she punctuated each word with spittle as she spat them out. "I am human! Mom and Dad were my real parents."

"They were our parents," Amell agreed. "To a point. The embryo they created was a combination of genes injected microscopically. We were grown in a petri dish before being inserted in Mom's wound for a real human pregnancy scenario. My animal blend is predominantly lion. Yours is multiple, including chimpanzee, elephant and dolphin. We're not sure which is your dominant gene."

"How do you know this?" she challenged. "How can you tell what I am when I don't even show any physical resemblance to any of those animals. I don't have a long snout for a nose or big floppy ears."

"Well," Amell chuckled softly, taking a tentative step toward his sister. "Your ears are on the large side. As is your nose. Remember, I used to tease you about it? The other animal traits probably lessened the elephant physical attributes."

Priya marched right up to Amell and smacked him on the chest. If anyone else had dared, Amell would have reacted. Not Priya. Not his younger sister. He was honor bound to defend her, not attack her. "I need answers, Amell." She stood on her tiptoes to bring her face inches from his. Looking deep into his eyes, she held his gaze with intensity and determination. "I need answers," she repeated, "not teasing."

Amell took her hands in his before she could smack him again. "And you shall have answers. It is time you knew everything. At least the extent of the answers as we know them here at Castle Mutasim." Tucking one of her arms under his, he made way to the passageway beyond the conservatory. "I'll take you to the library. I can show you the documents we've secured as well as answer as many of your questions as I can."

Keeping pace with Amell, she sniffled softly. "Mom? Dad? Did they know?" She asked, her voice feeble, as if she wasn't sure she wanted to know.

"They were scientists, Priya," Amell answered. "They worked on the program as well as volunteered their services." He held up his free hand to ward off her complaints. "Gross. I know. But they firmly believed in their science. In their research. In creating the perfect living creature. One that was brilliant, incredibly strong, and with a long lifespan. The records I've secured document their work. Their ongoing battles to keep us, you and me, in their care. And the final orders…"

"They were murdered, weren't they?" Priya asked, gasping as the pain of this sudden realization sending sharp arrows through her body.

"Yes. It would seem so."

They reached another set of pocket doors, finely polished wood which slithered into the walls with ease. Priya maintained her hold of Amell, stifling a gasp as they entered. "Wow!" was all she could say. She had seen images of impressive libraries around the world: the Strahov Monastery Library in the Czech Republic with more than 200,000 books and incredible ceiling frescoes, the Trinity College Library in Ireland which held the incredible *Book of Kells*, the George Peabody Library in Baltimore, and so many others. The libraries were works of art in themselves; not to mention the shelves of classics each revered space preserved for all time. Priya had visited some of them, including the one in Ireland.

But this? Amell's library? Castle Mutasim's library? It was far superior to all of the others on the planet in so many ways.

"Wow!" she half-whispered, voicing her sense of awe and wonder with reverence. "How?"

Amell chuckled softly. "We'll save that question for later. Why don't we start with you and me? Our ancestry? Our roots? Who we are and where we originated? There are a lot of how's and why's in that discovery alone to satisfy you for many days."

He patted her arm, the one still tucked under his. "Come." He led her forward. "I have everything laid out on the table by the window. You must let me show you and explain to you what I know. What all of us here at the castle know."

"First," Priya held back. "Please tell me where here is."

He paused briefly before leading her toward the far end of the table littered with papers, documents of all sorts, and laptops.

There was a map of the world laid out; pins pricking various locations, like a war plan layout. He pointed. "We're here."

"But," she stammered in response. "You had me drive to Skagway. This is nowhere near Skagway. And what are all those other pins?"

CHAPTER TEN

Priya studied the point on the map where Amell's finger rested. She muttered the names of the villages nearby, "Tahsis. Gold River. Strathcona Park is just south of here. But why Vancouver Island? In the middle of the island, no less. Cut off from roads to the main centers. And why the ruse to get me up north? To Yukon?"

"First." Amell stepped away from the table and started pacing. "We had to lose the trail."

"Of the so-called bad guys," she filled in the gaps.

"Yes." He maintained a steady pace as he walked around the table. "And, we had to take you far enough away from our location, remove your implant and make sure all was secure from the contents of your car. The car remains where you drove off the mountain. They'll be combing the area for months, looking for you and Bear." He cleared his throat. "I mean Wayne."

"Implant? What implant?"

"We all had implants installed when we were born," Amell explained, his patience wearing thin as Priya's questions morphed into multiple tangents before any were adequately addressed. "To keep track of us, should we go rogue or be abducted. There's big business in buying and selling our bodies, both live and dead. Every superpower on the planet is intent on creating the newest, fiercest, most powerful living creature. Superhero soldiers. We didn't want you leading the enemy troops to our doorstep. Each one of us has had the implant removed, surgically, before we are allowed settle here. It's a matter of security. For everyone here."

"But I wasn't aware of any implant. Or its removal, for that matter."

"None of us were," Amell explained. "Until something happened, or we connected with another being who had been on the run for some time. We connected with others and helped each other." He paused briefly to clear his throat. "Wayne removed the implant while you slept in that dreadful dump in Prince George." He held up his hands in mock surrender. "His words, not mine."

"Humph!" Priya grunted in response. She hadn't given up on her questions. Not by a long shot. "Why didn't you rescue me sooner?" Priya's eyes glazed over as she pondered the multiple times she suspected being watched. Being followed. She shuddered at the memories. She had even reported a few cases to the police, but nothing came of the reports. She gave up reporting. No point.

"You were always under our watchful eyes," Amell made a feeble attempt to reassure her. "We sent you Wayne to watch out for you. To care for you. He will share his stories of what transpired while you were at work or out visiting friends, shopping, whatever. We weren't entirely sure you were one of us. We didn't know how much brainwashing they'd managed to do to you. We wanted to observe their actions to gain a better idea. With Wayne's reports, our concern increased, and we decided it was time to bring you here."

Pacing the room, circling the table in the opposite direction of Amell who continued his pacing, she pondered aloud, "I still don't understand how I couldn't have known I was *different*."

"They had created something in you that made you blend in better than the rest of us," Amell explained. The two pacing figures crossed each other and continued their trajectory in opposite directions. "A super being that appeared, acted and did everything in an entirely human way. You were the first. Their biggest success. They were studying you, looking for flaws, waiting for the right time to take you back to the lab. To allow you to explore your other genes. And there were others watching, too.

Rogue nations. Rogue labs. All seeking the best test subject. You."

"But why didn't I know?" She stopped abruptly and leaned on the table, glaring across at Amell, who had also come to a standstill.

He shrugged his shoulders. "I can only surmise, Priya. Perhaps by not knowing, you could play out the part of being totally human. They were testing you, Priya. As they tested all of us in one way or another."

"So, what now?" She waved her hands over the table surface, taking in all the material she surmised was laid out for her to study. To understand. Or not. "I stay here forever. Hiding. What kind of a life is that?"

"The only other option is to live with them. Living in a lab. Under constant scrutiny. Being prodded and poked and tested to the nth degree. Or used as their toy. To obstruct justice. To destroy others."

She let out a deep sigh of frustration. Allowing her hands to rest again on the table, her eyes rivetted, focussed on her hands, studying them closely. Different. She was different. Like Amell. Like Kat. Like Bear (no Wayne, she must remember). Like Roderick. Like all the others. Glancing up, she noticed Amell hadn't resumed his pacing and was standing still as a statue, watching her every move.

"Why here? It's so isolated."

"Exactly the point. We're far enough away from civilization that those people who seek our imprisonment won't think to look here. We're close enough to Tahsis, which is accessible to the outside world, to get what supplies we need. We do get the occasional hiker seeking nature's refuge. If they get too curious, we take them in and treat them with a mind-numbing drug, so they can't remember us or our location. Perfectly harmless. Then we set them loose on a trail far from here, but near enough to Tahsis that they can find their way back."

"I have vague recollections of the rescue," Priya pondered, eyes focused on her brother. "I felt like I was strapped into something, like a dog sled. And dragged along the ground."

"We had to transport you to the chopper, down the mountain range you were climbing," Amell explained.

"Wouldn't there be tracks?"

"All buried thanks to the late spring storm that swept across the region."

"And yet it was safe enough to fly a chopper in to rescue me?"

"No. But we had to try."

Kat entered the library, breaking the stalemate of blunt questions and answers. "Amell." Her voice sounded silky when she addressed Priya's brother. She walked over to the table and looped an arm through Amell's.

"You're a couple," Priya stated what was now obvious.

"Yes." Amell and Kat answered in unison.

"What if…?" Priya couldn't finish.

"What if we have children?" Kat finished the question for Priya. "We do. Two. A boy and a girl. George and Amelie. Age nine and six. I'll introduce you later."

"But…?"

"And they look perfectly normal." Kat air quoted the last word. "I should say, they look human."

"Only time will tell," Amell added. "Many of us don't demonstrate our uniqueness until our teens or later. You didn't even notice yours. And neither did your human friends and colleagues."

Priya pondered the new knowledge. Amell and Kat. Children of two parents each with mixed human and animal genes. How widespread was this duplicity? Was there no longer such a creation as a pure human being?

"Possibly not," Kat answered Priya's unasked question. Noticing the surprised look, she quickly added, "I read minds. It's part of the cat gene in me. Sorry." Her face reflected remorse. "I try to control the urge, but sometimes I can't. You have such an open mind, Priya. Part of your gift, I suppose. But one you'll have to learn to control. For your own safety."

"In case I confront the monsters who created us?" Priya asked with grave concern dripping from her sarcasm.

"Exactly," Amell agreed. "But right now, you need to know all there is to know, or at least all we know to share, about who and what we are."

He moved toward the end of the table with the map. "These pins," he waved a hand over the surface, "represent each facility around the world, the ones we know about, which are experimenting and creating living beings of mixed genes. All for various nefarious purposes."

"There must be thousands," Priya moved over, standing on the opposite side of the table from Amell. She glanced intently at the map. "At least three in Canada. All up north."

"And all owned and operated by foreign enterprises," Amell added. "One thing Canadians do well is give up our rights to anything and everything of value."

"Like the oil sands," Priya concluded. "Like our water."

"And so much more." Kat had moved, taking up position at the end of the table, between Amell and Priya. Like a referee, she stood guard, glancing first at one then the other. "You have no idea how little Canada actually controls. Or owns, for that matter."

"It'll come to a fore at some point," Amell continued. "But right now, we have our own concerns to address." He moved down the table, the others following him. "I suggest you start with these documents, Priya." He pointed to a stack of papers. "We could search records online, but we have to be careful not to leave a trace. We avoid using the internet and cellular devices. Speaking of which," he glanced at his sister, "we left your cell phone and laptop in the car. Wayne removed the tracers as best he could, but we didn't want to take a chance he missed something. Your friends in Victoria have been compromised, so it's not safe to contact them. Should you wish to write an old-fashioned letter, you may do so and one of our runs to the outside will drop it in the mail, far from here."

"But how can they write back?" Priya asked. "I know Samantha will be terribly worried. She didn't want me to come here in the first place. Or, at least, where we both believed here," she air quoted the word, "was. She's my best friend. My only friend."

"And an operative," Kat interjected. "A spy."

"What!" Priya exclaimed. "No. It can't be."

"But it is," Amell agreed with his partner. "How well do you truly know this Samantha person? Do you know where she lives? Where she works? How did you meet?"

"I think I know her well enough," Priya stumbled over her answer. "No. I don't know where she lives. I have her cell number and we make plans over the phone to meet for lunch or dinner. I thought she worked for the government, but I'm not sure where her office is. We met by chance a few years ago. I was walking around the inner harbor during my lunch break, and we just struck up a conversation and discovered we had so much in common."

"Don't you find that a little bit strange?" Kat asked.

"No more than being here and learning that I'm different. That I'm a lab rat."

"You're anything but a lab rat," Amell grumbled. "We're all more than mere lab rats. And it's time they, the lab techies, realized it."

"We'll leave you for now," Kat suggested, giving her partner's arm a gentle tug. "I know there's a lot of information to sort through. If you have any questions, think them. I'll hear you, try to answer as much as I can and join you if you need me. Otherwise, we'll plan to fetch you for lunch, which always tends to be a rowdy affair amongst our motley group of misfits." She chuckled softly. The other two grimaced.

Amell gave a soft, deep throated growl, then spoke, "Kat's right. Even if we don't like the term. What these monsters have done is create a disposable army of misfits and superpowered creations."

"Are humans even that intelligent to create such creatures?" Priya glanced at the two, but they averted her gaze. "You don't think…" Her eyebrows shot up. "Aliens?"

"It has to be," Kat whispered. "Human engineering isn't a strong part of human intelligence. But they're probably part of the problem."

"The slaves of the lab," Amell snorted. He waved to the pile of documents. "Read. Study. Save questions for later. See you at lunch." And the two left the library before Priya could think of another question to ask.

Pulling out a chair, she sat, prepping herself for a morning of slogging through heavy reading material. Human genetics wasn't one of her favorite genres, but she had to find the answers. Somewhere. Somehow. Staring at the pile wouldn't make it go away. Neither could her mind absorb the contents in this manner.

Although she was blessed with a powerful photographic memory, she had to actually look at the documents before her brain could snap the image and process the contents. The thousands of pages on the table in front of her, all fine print by the looks of it, would take her the morning. No more. No less. Anyone else, it would take days. Working in the archives, she was efficient in her work, but she struggled to control her unusual abilities. She endured the pet name her colleagues gave her: Biblioprocessor. They meant well, but she didn't want them to be too aware of how quickly she could absorb pages of information.

Thinking back, she was starting to realize she had been aware of something uniquely different about her. She was actually brilliant. Not like Einstein by any means. But she did have certain talents which no one else had. She had read about photographic memory. It was real. But her photographic memory was like a rapid speed photocopier. If not faster.

It took her little over an hour to plow through what would take normal homo sapiens weeks to read, let alone process. She was reaching the bottom of the pile of documents when her hands stopped, and her eyes stared blatantly at the page.

In a soft voice she read aloud, "Specimen number 20259. Name given: Priya Moore. Born: March 1, 1990." She gasped. "That's me!" Her eyes glazed over. With a deep inhalation, she continued. "Parents, Alyssa and Jeremy Moore. Older sibling

Amell Moore. Other siblings rejected." She stopped abruptly. Other siblings? She had a larger family than merely Amell and herself? She'd have to ask him. Reading on, she hoped to discover more, but was disappointed to merely read a list of her mutant makeup. "Genetic makeup: forty percent human, ten percent each of chimpanzee, elephant and dolphin." She stopped again and studied the last entry. "Chimpanzee? Really? Why? How?" She continued reading, "I'm a real mishmash of this and that. But what about the remaining thirty percent?" She quickly scanned the documents but found nothing to indicate what the remaining thirty percent comprised. She read on, "Genetic bonding fused well and result quite satisfying. May be best specimen yet. Very human looking. No visual signs of mutant genetics. Only the large black patch, like a mole or a birthmark, on left thigh. Easily hidden underneath clothing." Priya gasped, realizing they knew about her one deformity, as she called it.

She recalled her teen years, wanting to wear short shorts or sparse bikinis, frustrated her ugly spot would show. "It's a birthmark," her mother explained. "Some people might call it a beauty mark." To which she had responded, "Nothing beautiful about that blight on my skin. I have to wear the clothes of an old woman to cover it up." She couldn't understand her mother's answering chuckle. Priya had survived, avoiding swimming pools and beach parties, but it hadn't been easy. Once she was in her twenties, she no longer cared to wear revealing clothes.

She glared at the page before her. There was no doubt, now. This brief was about her. Mentioning the spot on her thigh proved it. She read the last few lines before flipping to the final page in the pile. "Will release into custody of Alyssa and Jeremy Moore along with older sibling, Amell, until such time as deemed necessary to bring her back for reprograming."

The last page was brief. Undated, but the contents suggested a known timeline. "Amell Moore has disappeared without a trace. No signal from implant. Must have been removed. Parents, Alyssa and Jeremy Moore to be annihilated once Priya is old enough to care for herself. Will continue monitoring. Too soon to bring her in. She must consume as much human knowledge as possible first."

She slapped the last page on top of the pile and banged her palms on the table. "They killed my parents. They were using us all." She was angry. Extremely angry.

"Calm yourself." Kat was there as she placed the last page upside down on top of the others. She knew. Kat could read minds, so she would be aware of Priya's completion of phase one of the research. If she was paying attention, which she obviously was. "We won't accomplish anything through anger."

"But they murdered my parents!" Her eyes glossed over with tears not shed since the accident which took their lives. "Murdered them!" she reiterated in little more than a murmur.

"Lunch," Kat stated simply. "They are all waiting. Amell wants to make formal introductions, so you know everyone. Then we'll eat. You must be starving. I know I am."

She didn't wait for an answer, merely pivoting around and heading for the door. Priya, with her stomach surprisingly in a growling rage, stood up and followed Kat, the anger dissipating as she anticipated a hearty meal. *How can I be so hungry after eating such a huge breakfast only a few hours ago?*

You're mutating. Kat answered inside Priya's head. Not only could Amell's mate hear Priya, but she could also communicate with her telepathically as well. *It's the cat gene in me.* She answered Priya's question before the girl could think it.

"Mutants," Priya grumbled, loud enough for her ears only.

Kat heard. "Mutants we are," she called over her shoulder. "And pretty damn proud of it, too."

As the two made their way toward the dining room, they were almost barrelled over by a mob of youngsters. Priya flattened herself against the wall, allowing them space, allowing her time to study the faces as they blurred past. They appeared human enough. Which ones were Amell and Kat's?

Kat chuckled, answering inside Priya's mind. *The two ringleaders, of course. Would you expect anything else?* Then she called out in a voice louder than Priya would have expected, "George. Amelie. Come here. Now. And bring your followers with you."

The group slithered to a halt, sliding into one another as their momentum only slowed slightly. There were a few ouches and comments like, "Watch out," but the group refrained from elbowing and causing a scuffle. With a stern clearing of the throat, Kat had their attention, and the troop meekly made their way back, George and Amelia in the lead.

Eyes downcast, the young people awaited the discipline they knew was coming. "Now children," Kat began, then changed her tone. "George and Amelie," she lightly scolded, "you should know better. Racing around the halls, especially on the main floor is forbidden."

"Yes, Mother," they answered in unison, their tone reflective of a combination of remorse and a desire to challenge the edict.

"Yes, Miss Kat," the others muttered their responses.

"There is too much activity on the main floor, and you could cause yourself serious injury," she continued with the scolding. "That's why the top floor and the roof have been allocated as your play area."

"But, Mother," Amelie, who didn't look much older than six, replied with meek reverence. "We've already done that. Many times. The floors upstairs aren't as polished as these floors and there's no challenge." She spoke with the language of someone much older, although her bouncing blond curls suggested she was still quite young.

"Rules are rules, Amelie." Kat reached down and took her daughter gently by the shoulders. "You know why we have these rules?"

Amelie glanced briefly at her mother, allowing her eyes to dart sideways to her older brother before nodding her head. "Yes, Mother."

"Father says rules are made to be broken," George announced boldly. He was a few inches taller than his sister, with light brown, wavy hair which suggested he might morph into a mutant like his father. Too early to tell.

A clearing of a male voice from down the hall stopped further discussion on rules. "George. Amelie. You know better." It was Amell. He approached the group. "As do all of you young people. Now, before we go in for lunch, you have someone to meet. George. Amelie. This is my younger sister, your Aunt Priya. Please make her feel welcome."

Priya was suddenly swarmed by young people. Amelie, obviously not shy, immediately swung her arms around Priya's waist and gave a welcoming hug. "I always wanted an aunt," she declared. "And you look just like me." She did, too. Priya hadn't noticed before, but there was definitely a resemblance. She'd have to dig out her childhood photos and compare them to this young treasure.

"I've always wanted a niece," she answered with a warm smile. Glancing at George, who held back, too dignified to be overly demonstrative, she added, "And a nephew."

There were more greetings as all the children took the opportunity to introduce themselves to Miss Priya, as they called her.

"Now children." Kat clapped her hands. "Let's go in for lunch."

As Kat promised, lunch was a raucous event. After the introductions to the children, their parents and the other mutants, Priya's head was swimming, not just from the information she'd processed, but by all the names she'd heard. She already knew Wayne (formerly her Bear) and Roderick. Kat and Amell, too, of course. There was also a Guinevere, Suzanna, Michaela, Horace and so many other names. Fortunately, as well as her photographic memory, Priya had an instant audio memory as well. She remembered everything she heard. In great detail. And she was able to process the names and faces into one single file for each person, or mutant, tucking the information safely and categorically away for future reference. She was, after all, a trained librarian.

Unlike breakfast, which had platters lined up on the sideboard, lunch consisted of platters of bread, sandwiches, several kinds of cheeses and fruit, all situated at various intervals along the table. Everyone reached for what they wanted. When a platter emptied, whoever took the last morsel took responsibility for replacing it with another heaping platter from the sideboard.

However, like breakfast, everyone consumed massive amounts of food. Even the children. Even Priya. She couldn't remember ever having such a voracious appetite.

CHAPTER TWELVE

Amelie had taken an instant liking to her new aunt and insisted on sitting with her. The other children were interspersed amongst the grownups, presumably sitting as family units. George had claimed a seat between his parents, while Amelie sat between Priya and Wayne. Amelie didn't speak much, but she ate with a voracious appetite which matched the others, all while silently observing the newest addition to the family out of the corner of her eye. The others were not so quiet, wanting to interrogate Priya about herself and what she'd learned during the morning study period.

"So, what did you learn this morning?" Once again, Wayne asked, projecting his voice over the head of the little girl who sat between them. It was the closest he could sit to Priya, as Amell, sitting at the head of the table, claimed his sister's other side. Wayne appeared intent to hold true to his duty of being her BFF. Only Wayne was no longer Priya's rescued dog, Bear. He was a mutant like everyone else seated at the table. Herself included.

"Too much," Priya summarized in two words. She shoveled another mouthful of food into her mouth and chewed thoughtfully before adding, "I feel like my brain is ready to burst. How can people do this to living beings? It makes me so mad!" She dropped her utensils with a clatter and banged a fist on the table.

Silence erupted, if such a thing could happen. Everyone froze, eyes glued on Priya, the source of the outburst. Amell broke the silence, "We all feel that way, Priya. Only some of us have had more time to get used to the idea of being what others would describe as a mutant."

"But how long has this been going on?" she demanded. "Years? Decades? Centuries? I didn't think humans had the know-how to do this considering it wasn't that long ago scientists, human scientists, created the first cloned lamb." She was referring, of course, to Dolly, cloned in 1996.

"What makes you think it was humans who engineered all of us?" Roderick cast a wary glance her way. "It's been going on for centuries and history is full of stories of strange beings roaming the earth."

"Aliens?"

"Quite possibly," Roderick took the lead. He paused, glancing at Amell for permission to continue.

Amell nodded. "Go ahead, Roderick. You're the expert in this field of research. Just remember there are young ears at the table, so keep it simple." He was referring to the children, but they didn't appear concerned. Quite the opposite. Their eyes lit up at the possibility of a story, one which included aliens and monsters and mutants and secret labs. Not having seen normal human adults in the outside world, Castle Mutasim was more than a refuge to them. It was their home. The only home they'd ever known.

Casting a look around the room at the eager young eyes giving him their full attention, Roderick shook his head slightly, a coy smile tugging at the corners of his mouth. He glanced briefly at Amell and said, "I don't think we need worry about the young ears. They've seen more than most children their age." Amell waved a hand to suggest he carry on. Roderick returned his attention to Priya, shoving his now empty plate aside and placing his elbows on the table, cupping his hands so he could drop his chin in the palms, if you could call them palms. He was obviously settling in for the long story. "It goes way back in human history," he began. "The First Nations, the First Peoples, the Aboriginals, whatever is the correct terminology for the geographic region or for the current time for that matter. Anyway, their stories, legends, totems and art all reflect on animal spirituality – some sort of connection with the animal world. Even the Chinese have their connections to the animal world: every year is the Lunar Year of some animal. For example, this year is the Chinese Lunar Year of the Goat. Now, back to the Aboriginals worldwide. Anthropologists and historians started referring to this connection as anthropomorphism, the merging of human characteristics with that of animals. Some sentient beings believed they morphed into their animal counterpart at certain times of the day, the month or the year."

He paused long enough to take a sip of water. Priya took the opportunity to speak. "So, anthropomorphism is not just a legend. It's a reality."

Roderick placed his glass on the table and resumed his position, leaning more heavily into the palms of his hands. "Very much so. You can't tell me that these creatures merely appear in one's imagination worldwide, throughout history. Even cavemen drew stick representations that could be interpreted as anthropomorphism."

"Human and animal," Priya finished the thought.

"Take the Kwakwaka'wakw, for example," Roderick continued. "There's a village not far from here, Gwa'yasdams, on one of the many islands between Vancouver Island and the mainland. It's mostly deserted now, at least the beach where totems guarded the entrance depicting a woman/cat creature they called D'Sonoqua. She, or it, was a giantess, featured prominently in much of the mythology of the Kwakwaka'wakw peoples of Vancouver Island. Huge and scary. Believed to ward off evil spirits, hence the totems of D'Sonoqua in villages, but also evil. Parents warned their young ones of D'Sonoqua. Like the wicked witch in the Hansel and Gretel fairy tale, D'Sonoqua would kidnap children and they were never seen again."

"Perhaps they were taken to these alien laboratories for research, conversion, whatever they do," Priya suggested.

"Exactly," Roderick nodded enthusiastically. "I should take you to Gwa'yasdams to see these D'Sonoqua totems for yourself. What remains of them. D'Sonoqua still prowls the forests of northern Vancouver Island. I'm sure of it. And other creatures, too. Like Sasquatch."

"Bigfoot."

"And others."

Amell cleared his throat. "Enough for now. I think lunch is over. We all have our duties to see to. Wayne," he faced Priya's one-time faithful companion. "Why don't you finish the tour of the facilities – inside and out."

Wayne stood up, stretching to his full length. Clothed, now, he only had traces of his former self as Priya's rescued dog, Bear. Mostly in the eyes. "Priya," he held out his hand, still fur-covered and paw-like. "Shall we?"

"Can I come, too?" Amelie spoke up, her voice soft and velvety like her mother's.

"Amelie," Kat appeared at her side. "You have lessons this afternoon. You'll see your aunt again later.

"Why don't you give me a tour of the top floor and rooftop later?" Priya bent down to meet her niece at eye level. "You can show me your room and your special places."

Amelie appeared satisfied. "Okay." She gave a brief response before she trotted off to join the other children.

"You've made another friend, Priya," Wayne congratulated her. "You always did have a soft touch for children. And now you have a niece who adores you at first glance. Like I did." The last three words were almost a whisper, but Priya heard them. And her cheeks flushed in response.

CHAPTER THIRTEEN

There wasn't much else to tour on the main floor. Or so Wayne claimed. She had seen the conservatory and the massive library. She had eaten in the grand dining room. It only left what might be called the living room or drawing room. "We call it our living space," Wayne summarized it. "We don't receive visitors. Only new additions to our family, like you. So, this is where we live, play, relax, breathe."

Priya glanced around quickly, taking in the large screen television, the ping pong table, card tables, plush rugs and soft cushioned couches and chairs. A massive hearth sat in the center of the outer wall, unlit since it was still early in the day. "Looks more like a playroom to me," she remarked. "I bet the children love it."

Wayne merely chuckled, "Right. Only they're not allowed in here without adults to supervise. They have their own play areas." He led her along the grand hall away from the playroom, away from the grand staircase, toward the thick wooden, double doors, presumably the grand entrance.

"Amell's architecture, I presume," she muttered. "He always did have a romantic, medieval flare to his creativity."

"We all wanted a medieval castle," Wayne responded, yanking the cross bar and pulling one of the doors inward. "And this is what we built. It may look medieval and have so many medieval characteristics, but it's state-of-the-art, high tech twenty-first century."

"Wired for sound, light, intrusion and whatever else you can imagine," Priya added glibly.

"Exactly." He motioned Priya through the door and he followed, pulling the door closed behind him.

The air outside was fresh. Priya couldn't resist the urge to breathe deeply. "It smells like pine and cedar and all a forest should smell like after a brisk clean rain."

"Or a heavy snow," Wayne agreed. "There was a lot of snow overnight, but it's since melted. The warmth of the sun quickly erased any traces of a late winter snowfall. Typical of the west coast rainforest, rain and snow. Always damp. It's just beyond the castle ramparts." Wayne pointed at the tall, brick and mortar construction marking the outer perimeter. "Inside the walls, we are safe from the outside world. As safe as we can be. We take turns patrolling, either monitoring the electronic sensors or walking along the ramparts. Once you settle in, you'll be given your own rotation schedule."

Wayne gently took Priya by the elbow and led her away from the castle, into the manicured lawns and gardens, some pristine and orderly like an English country garden at a grand noble home, just waiting for spring to arrive and stay, to make things glow with brilliant colors. Other spaces were left rugged, allowed to grow in a more natural state. As they moved away from the castle, Priya chanced a few glances back to marvel at the edifice.

"It's massive!" she exclaimed on more than one occasion. "I've only seen the main floor and part of the second floor. The kitchens, I presume, are below ground level," Wayne nodded in response. "But there must be two, three more floors of space. And turrets and towers to boot. For what purpose?"

"We all have our own private living space," Wayne explained. "So, we can be human or transform to our animal self. The turrets and towers," he pointed at one corner then another, "are for the birds of prey, so they can venture out whenever they feel the need to soar above the trees. The top floor is for those with gorilla and chimpanzee genes so they can trample the rooftop, and swing down to the nearest grove of tress when the mood arises."

"And the children?" Priya asked. "I thought they had command of the top floor."

"They do," Wayne agreed. "At the rear of the castle. An entire unit is sealed off from the rest of the castle and its inhabitants, in case one of the mutants goes rogue and causes dangerous mischief."

"And where does that place you?" Priya glanced coyly at the dogman. She blinked, drew in a breath quickly, trying to grapple her senses. What was she doing? Flirting? She'd never flirted before. And with Wayne, once known as Bear? Something was off.

Wayne merely rewarded her with a warm smile. "On the second floor, not far from your room." The two stood rooted, facing the castle, but not looking at it, their eyes locked on each other.

"What have we here?" Roderick interrupted the moment and Priya stepped back suddenly. Wayne coughed and turned away. "Well. Well. Never mind. We have other things to address. There's been a breach."

Wayne was immediately all business. "Where?" he demanded.

"Approaching the south wall," Roderick replied. "Sissy has been tracking the person's approach." He was referring to the bald eagle/ human mutant Priya had met along with the others. Turning to Priya, "She's our best scout. Don't know what we'd do without her." As if sensing Priya's unease, he quickly added, "Don't worry about the children, Priya. They're safe and secure in their space. And those not needed are serving to protect our most vulnerable: our children."

"Yes," Priya agreed readily. "The children must be protected at all costs. They would make easy victims of these scientific experiments."

"As well we know that, Priya," Roderick added. "Wayne, your assistance is needed."

"Of course, but one question." He took his time to study Roderick intently before asking. "Why didn't the alarm sound?"

Roderick shrugged his shoulders. "We don't know." Turning to Priya, he added, "We have an alarm that goes off when there's a breech. To warn everyone and make sure everyone is where they should be, and all is secure. It appears," he cleared his throat, allowing his eyes to roam from Priya to Wayne and back to Priya, "that our system has been compromised and the alarm disengaged. If Sissy hadn't noticed the intruders, we'd be in dire circumstances right now." He turned abruptly. "No time for further chit chat. Priya, you must return to your rooms until all is secure. Wayne. With me."

Before turning to follow Roderick, Wayne addressed Priya, "We'll continue the tour later. It might be best if you retreated into the castle while we deal with this intrusion."

"Can't I help?" she asked. She didn't like being brushed aside.

"Not this time," Wayne was blunt enough to ward off any disagreement. "You're still fragile. You've only been with us for a couple of days."

"You're just as fragile, Wayne. You were in the accident with me."

"But I've known my situation longer than you have and I've trained for these incidents. Now, please Priya." his voice took on a begging tone. "You must do as Roderick asks. This time."

Wayne reached out to take Priya's arm, presumably to lead her inside. She shook him off and marched toward the entrance on her own. She knew when she wasn't wanted. Or needed.

CHAPTER FOURTEEN

She could hear doors slamming shut, locks engaging. At least the locking system was still operational even if the sound alarm wasn't. The castle was going into total lockdown. What was out there? What was the threat?

Priya paced the halls of the main floor, studying again each room, taking in details she'd overlooked the first time. With her photographic memory, she knew the layout well from one mere walk-through and she knew most of the contents of each room. It didn't necessarily mean she didn't miss things. Like the way the wide screen television in what she'd dubbed the playroom, was on, displaying various venues around the castle, both inside and out. It was operating like a guardroom monitor. All along the halls and in each room were similar devices, monitoring both inside the enclosure and beyond the castle walls.

There was a flurry of activity in the halls and each room she attempted to enter. The playroom was packed, people standing or sitting, even some hanging from the walls and the ceiling. All eyes were glued to the screen. There was little space and she needed space. To herself. She wanted solitude. Quiet. Time to process all that was happening.

She felt a slight tug on her elbow and noticed Kat nodding further down the hall. "Come with me. We'll find you a quiet space." It was unnerving how Kat could read Priya's mind and sense her private thoughts and feelings.

"How can you…?" she started, then stopped herself. Kat might understand her given talent, but could she explain it to Priya in a comprehensible manner?

Kat was scurrying down the hall. "Amell and the others are outside the walls, securing the person, or persons, we don't know how many yet, who's breached our protective space. While we wait indoors, we watch. We observe. And we all know when and if we're needed. For now, we stay secure and watch." She opened the door to the conservatory and motioned Priya inside. "You'll be at peace here. No one will disturb you."

"But the children," Priya protested before Kat could leave. She sensed the other's anxiety about the events taking place. The unknown. The ongoing fear of being captured and returned to the lab. For more tests. For more experiments.

"They're fine." Kat's voice sounded amazingly calm. "I'm going to be with them now."

"Shall I join you?" As much as Priya wanted to be alone, she also wanted to be with others. She felt a strong pull toward the children, especially her niece, Amelie.

She was rejected, however. Kat shook her head. "No. I'll go. You're still someone new to them. They might not feel comfortable with you around. In the given unsettled circumstances." She nodded to the piano. "You stay here. Play. Make some music. It'll permeate through the walls and soothe us all." Before Priya could say anything else, Kat had vanished. Quite literally.

"It must be the cat in her," Priya muttered under her breath.

Absolutely. Came the coy response inside her head.

With a chuckle, mostly to ease the building tension, Priya walked across the threshold, taking a seat at the piano, an activity which had soothed her through so many events in her life. How she had missed this piano. Missed her music.

She ran her fingers across the keyboard and started playing some technical exercises: scales, chords, arpeggios. Breathing deeply, she felt herself melting into the tones of the music. If it was possible. She was instantly jolted from her reverie by a small voice at her side.

"Will you teach me to play?"

Priya jumped up, almost shrieking. When her heart settled, she gasped. "Amelie. What are you doing here? You should be upstairs with the children. Your mother will be worried."

"She knows where I am," the young girl proclaimed with a tone of nonchalance. "She always does. Just as she knows where you are. And what you're thinking."

The two exchanged smiles, the tension easing. "It's the cat in her, I guess," they said together, then laughed.

As the chuckles eased, Amelie shrugged her shoulders. "I've been with you all along. I followed you outside and back."

"You did, did you?" Priya studied the girl intently, trying to mask a serious look. It failed and the two broke out into another bout of laughter.

Clearing her throat, Priya responded to the girl's request. "Yes. I'll teach you how to play the piano. It'll be my pleasure. But first, shall I play something for you?"

Amelie nodded. "Can you play some animal songs? I like music that sounds like an animal."

"Any particular animal?"

"Elephant," came the emphatic reply.

"How about this?" And Priya launched into the piano arrangement of Saint-Saëns' *The Elephant* from his famous *Carnival of the Animals.* "You have to imagine a deep bass melody, traditionally played by the double bass. That was Saint-Saëns original intent."

Amelie chuckled. "That does sound like an elephant." When Priya finished playing, the little girl instantly added another request, "Kangaroo!"

"Ah!" Priya chuckled. "You like the animals from Saint-Saëns arrangements I see." And she started playing an arrangement for one piano, from the original which was intended for two pianos.

The girl was chuckling again. "I can hear the kangaroos jumping all over the place."

"My turn to choose," Priya announced. "How about something beautiful and elegant. Like a swan." And, without waiting for a response, she started playing the sweet-sounding melody, which Saint-Saëns intended for the harp.

When she finished, Amelie clapped her hands with delight. "That's so-o-o-o pretty." She elongated the 'so' to fully express her opinion. "Now. Teach me. I want to play."

And Priya did. The two were so engrossed in their teacher-student mode, they didn't notice the screen shots of the breach. They didn't notice the door open quietly. They didn't see Amell slip into the conservatory.

They were alone in their own little world of music. Or were they? Were they still being monitored by Kat? Even when they were alone? There was a monitor in the conservatory, just as there had been in the other rooms. The screen was following the events beyond the fortified walls surrounding the castle. It was a take-down, if that's what you could call it, of whatever breach had caused the lockdown.

And it was the scream which alerted Priya. It was as if she recognized the voice, if one could depict whose scream belonged to whom. She stopped her lesson and glanced at the monitor, not realizing her brother hovered near the door. Attention glued to the screen; she studied the event with great intensity. Her eyes had the capability of zooming in, like a camera. She made sense with her photographic memory. She zoomed in on the creature being pursued, the one who had caused the breach. It was human, or at least humanoid. It was in escape mode, crashing through the thick forest overgrowth. The noise was deafening as the pursuers, the castle residents, trampled toward it from all directions. When the creature turned, Priya captured a clear view of the face and gasped.

"Maurice?" she exclaimed. She was referring to a young man she met several months ago. She and Samantha had finished their ritual lunch together and Priya was heading back to her apartment. The two had literally bumped into one another, a conversation ensued complete with apologies and laughter. Maurice introduced himself as a bookseller. As they stood on the busy, tourist condensed streets of downtown Victoria, they talked about books. Maurice finally suggested they have tea at the Empress – his suggestion. She agreed and they enjoyed a long afternoon together, talking about themselves and about books. A relationship developed and they saw each other frequently, until one day, Priya was feeling ill and made the painful decision to call off their planned date. When she tried to look up the number for his bookstore, Passion For Books, she couldn't find a listing. Dragging herself out of the apartment, she ventured down to Government Street, where he claimed to run the store, only to discover the address he'd given didn't exist. It was then she realized she'd been duped. Heartbroken, she trundled back home, huddled on the couch wrapped in blankets to stem the shivers of whatever flu bug she was fighting, nursing a mug of steaming lemon tea doused with honey.

She considered sharing her sorrows with Samantha, but it would have required a lengthy dissertation on Maurice: who he was (or wasn't, as she'd just discovered) and how they'd met. As it turned out, she never did mention Maurice to Samantha. In fact, she didn't hear from her friend during the entire month she was dating Maurice.

When he phoned later to ask why she stood him up, she called him all sorts of names and ranted like an incoherent banshee, if there was such a thing. Then she hung up and turned off her phone. It was the last she heard from Maurice and the last she saw of him. Until now.

"What are you doing here?" she moaned in despair. "Have you been stalking me?" She desperately wanted to throw something at his image on the screen. Something. Anything. Except the precious music lying on the piano and in stacks on nearby tables.

Instead, she resorted to another of her actions of frustration: pounding the palms of her hand against the side of her head.

"Idiot! Idiot! Idiot!" she bewailed.

"You know this person?" It was Amell. She hadn't heard him enter the conservatory.

"Father!" Amelie squealed. Jumping from the piano bench and trotting over to her father, obviously hoping for a hug. "Aunt Priya is teaching me to play the piano."

"So I see." Amell's voice sounded stern. "You should be upstairs with the other children."

"But I want to be with my aunt," Amelie whined.

Kat appeared at that moment. "I'll take her upstairs, Amell." Nodding to her daughter, she said, "Come along Amelie." The two left without another word, though Amelie's sniffles could be heard as they made their way down the hall.

Alone with his sister, Amell repeated his question. "You know this person?"

Now sobbing, Priya confessed, "Yes. We dated a few months back. Until I discovered he was a fraud."

"He was and is." Amell approached the piano and slid onto the bench next to his sister. He wrapped an arm around her shoulders to comfort her as he had done so many times when she was younger. She leaned in and sobbed into his shoulder. "He's a spy for one of the labs. Which one, we don't know. But we shall soon find out." He reached for a remote and fast forwarded to another image. A woman. "As is she."

Through tear-stained eyes, Priya peaked at the screen and sobbed even harder. "Samantha?" she exclaimed. "My best friend? How could she?" Priya let out a wail and buried her head deeper in her brother's shoulder. "How could she?" she sobbed, nestling her head deeper into the shoulder.

Amell sat quietly, gently patting her shoulder as he had done years ago when Priya was distressed. As the sobbing abated, he continued to wait. Patience was one of his strong points. "Priya," he finally voiced in a subdued tone. "Priya. Look at me."

She hesitated. Sniffled. Pulled her head up and ran a sleeve across her face to wipe away the tears. "They're traitors, Amell," she stated in a drippy voice which was gaining power as anger seeped in, replacing the sorrow. "Traitors. How could they? Especially Samantha. She was my best friend. Forever."

"She's here, too, Priya." He tucked a finger under his sister's chin and raised her head a little more so he could gaze deep into her eyes. "Samantha is here, and she wants to talk to you. To see you."

"No!" She pulled back further, evidence of mounting anger sneaking across her face. "Absolutely not!"

"She might have some intel to help us, Priya," Amell stated, maintaining his calm. "All of us here have to put aside our feelings from time to time, for the good, safety and wellbeing of everyone living here." He stood up and walked around the piano, returning to stand in the curve of the instrument, facing Priya. "You don't have to see her right away. But think of what I said. You don't have to re-embrace her as a good friend. But you can listen to what she has to say and learn from it. Before we have her memories wiped."

"How did she find me, Amell?" Her tear-stained eyes glanced across to her brother, almost pleading. "How did they find me?"

"I don't know, Priya," Amell admitted. "I honestly don't know. We have people combing through your things now." Noticing his sister bristle at his comments, he held up his hands in surrender. "I had to, Priya. This could be the end of Castle Mutasim. Of us. All of us. There's more than just you at stake here, Priya."

He moved in closer and sat again on the bench next to Priya. Placing his index finger under her chin, once again he coaxed her head up so she would be looking deep into his eyes. It was something he always did to sooth her. Looking deep into her eyes, at this close a distance, had a powerful impact. Satisfied she was calming down slightly; he leaned forward and planted a brotherly kiss on her forehead. She couldn't help but smile at the sign of affection he'd often shown when she was a child.

"What now, Amell?" she asked, the sniffles still abating. "Do they have tracking implants?"

"Already removed. And Maurice has already had his memories wiped. He'll be dropped off somewhere on the mainland later today. One of our operatives will pick him up wandering aimlessly along a backroad and they'll drop him off as a John Doe at a local hospital. We'll do the same with Samantha. After you've talked to her, if that's what you decide to do."

Priya allowed her head to nod. "Not yet. Soon. I will, Amell. But not yet." She dropped her gaze to the piano keys. Music. It always soothed her.

Amell understood. "Play. Play your heart out, Priya. It'll help you think more clearly. It always did in the past."

CHAPTER FIFTEEN

"I heard you playing." The voice came from across the darkened room. Priya stood in the doorway, not sure whether to step into the room or make a dash for it. She had played hard and long on the piano, pounding out her frustrations, weaving tones into her emotional fragility. And she finally came. Here. To this room deep in the caverns of the earth.

Amell had led her down. Long spiralling staircases. Mazes of dark tunnels. He explained that intruders were taken to a safe underground facility far from the castle. To protect the edifice and its inhabitants. Deep enough in the earth and built like a bomb shelter bunker from the cold war. Signals from implants were lost, bouncing off the thick metal enclosure and the miles of dirt and rock in between. There were tunnels connecting the castle to this bunker prison, but even they were trick-wired, and maze constructed to confuse anyone not familiar with the layout. And Priya was definitely not familiar. She knew she couldn't run. She'd be lost in minutes. Amell led her here and he waited mere steps away for her to call out if she needed his help or she just wanted to return to the castle.

"Priya." The voice was Samantha's. Even in her weakened, semi-drugged state, it was still recognizable as her one-time friend. "Best friends." The voice cracked and a cough followed.

"No!" Priya finally found her voice. "You were never my friend. You deceitful, lying bitch!" She took a step toward the bed where Samantha's figure lay prone, barely moving. If there hadn't been a slow, steady rising and falling of the chest, Priya might have thought Samantha was dead. "How could you!" she wailed, as her steady progression led her to the foot of the bed. "How could you!" she repeated, venom spitting from her mouth with each word uttered. "How could you!" Always in threes. It was her number. Three. Even her anger came in three's.

"You are my friend, Priya." Samantha continued in a soft, strained voice. She lifted one hand as if reaching out to Priya. When she received no response, she allowed it to drop at her side. Releasing a deep sigh, she continued, "This began as a job, but you quickly wove a path into my heart. That's why they had to bring in Maurice. They no longer trusted me. I was not being fully disclosive in my reports. They knew I was holding back. My implants betrayed me in the end. Maurice was supposed to fill in the gaps. Only you were onto him too fast and that fizzled." She paused, turning away, coughing to clear her throat before finishing her speech. "Then you secured this job. They sent us out after you. We lost your trail up north then picked it up again here."

"How?" Priya demanded. She wanted to know more about their friendship, if it was real. However, there were more important issues at stake. "How did you find me? And so quickly?"

"They've developed a new, undetectable device," Samantha replied. "You remember the going-away gift I gave you?"

Priya nodded. "The book. The 1605 first addition of Cervantes *Don Quixote.* You boasted coyly that it cost you over $20,000. U.S. dollars, no less. I wondered then and wonder now, how you could afford that. And, as a going-away gift to a friend?"

"But you accepted it," Samantha pointed out.

"I did. With great reluctance. And now I wish I hadn't."

"You should have left it behind," her former friend admitted. "You remember the back cover? Where I showed you the bookbinder's clever fix-up job?" Priya nodded. "There's a paper-thin disk in there. Actually, it's thinner than paper. Can't see it. Can't feel it. Can't detect it. But they can trace it. And that's how we found you. Well, sort of. There's some sort of force field around your location blocking fully accurate transmission."

Priya stood quietly. Amell had mentioned the room would be bugged; she hoped they were unmasking the tracking device now they knew where it was. Finally. "You knew my passion for old books. For old stories about quests. You knew my passion in particular for the character of Don Quixote. And you took advantage of that."

"Not me," Samantha shook her head. "Them."

"Who's 'them'?" she demanded.

At first, silence met her question. Then, a slow, almost painful three-word response: "I don't know."

"What do you mean, you don't know?" Priya snapped. "How can you not know? You've always been super organized, super security crazy. This doesn't make sense."

"I don't remember before," Samantha explained. She tried to reach for her friend's hand again. Priya continued to refuse acknowledgement, standing frozen in her place at the end of the bed. "There's nothing before. I remember our first meeting, but nothing before that. It's strange. It's as if my mind was wiped and I don't understand how or why."

"And you never mentioned it before. Never questioned it."

Samantha shook her head slowly. "Other memories had been installed, but they didn't seem quite right, somehow." She paused briefly. "I have flashes of something else. Like a dream that disappears when you wake up in the morning, but little flashes appear throughout the day. It's very disturbing."

Priya was unsure how to answer. Perhaps her friend was as much a victim as she was. Or was this all part of the clever ruse to plague her and the others for years? She stepped back from the bed and paced the room, keeping her distance. Surely Kat would know, wouldn't she? Couldn't she look into Samantha's mind and see if it were true? Or would there be a danger to Kat to enter the predator's mind, one which was bugged by some superpower of unknown origins? She couldn't ask Kat. But, perhaps, she wouldn't have to. Kat would make her own decision on the matter. She was probably linked to Priya's thoughts this very minute. If only she could communicate with her through these brain connections.

You can. Priya nearly jumped. It was Kat's voice. In her head. She'd only known her brother's mate for a short time, but she had always been good at recognizing voices. *Yes. It's me, Priya. Trust your instincts. We'll run more tests before I do anything drastic. In the meantime, keep her talking. Perhaps she'll give us more clues. She did help us find the tracer in the book. Marvellous technology. The techies are studying it now. At a safe site where transmissions can't break the barriers. Now go! Talk to her. Tell her how disappointed you are. How frightened. Anything. Just don't reveal our location. Though they probably have a good idea already.*

Priya returned to her position at the end of the bed. "You know I don't forgive easily, Samantha. And I don't forget. You deceived me. I thought you were my friend. My only friend. And you deceived me." She was being harsh. She knew she was. It was working. Samantha squirmed under the bed covers.

"It wasn't me," she argued. "It was them. It was always them."

"What about your free will, Sammy?" The nickname she'd so often used slipped out from habit. "I always thought you were strong willed. Able to control your own thoughts and feelings."

"It was them," Samantha muttered again, sobs echoed in her protestations. "It was always them."

"So, what are you?" Priya demanded. "A robot? You can't be human if you have no free will." More harsh words.

"I am human." The prone figure spat, anger replacing the anguish.

"I don't think so," Priya countered. "I think you're a robot. A highly sophisticated one. Capable of making others, including myself, believe you are human. We'll know soon enough. Once they've completed their tests."

"No! You have to make them stop!"

"Why?"

"Because...." She struggled with her words, as if some part of her was instigating the power of free will. "I... will... self... destruct..."

Amell charged into the room. "Priya. Get out of here." He grabbed his sister's arm and tugged her toward the door as steam eschewed from Samantha's mouth, nose and ears.

"I... will... self... destruct..." The woman repeated over and over again in a mechanical voice, the room clouding into a thick mist with her steam. "I... will... self... destruct..."

Amell and Priya were coughing heavily as they ploughed through the door. Amell slammed it shut behind them and slapped a hand on a panel next to the door. "Engage," he yelled a command. Turning to Priya, he explained, "To protect the rest of the facility." He didn't get to say anything else as the room they had exited exploded, shaking the floors and walls where the two stood.

"Sammy! No!" Priya screamed, shaking off her brother's hold, trying valiantly to open the door, to re-enter, to save her friend. To do something. The door wouldn't budge. She pounded on it in frustration. "Sammy! No!" She sobbed, sinking to the floor, curling herself into a fetal bubble. "Sammy! Sammy!"

CHAPTER SIXTEEN

It was as before. She felt Amell lifting her off the ground and carrying her. She felt the comfort of being tucked into bed. And she sensed his caring presence.

The incessant sobbing had abated, leaving behind whimpers and chills and a growing numbness. It may have been hours; she lost track of time. When she finally did rejuvenate, enough to sit up unassisted, she noticed her brother sitting where he had previously after her rescue from the accident in a northern snowstorm.

"You must like the chair," she spoke quietly, her mouth grating as if it were full of sand. It didn't matter; the mere sound of her voice made him start. He shook his head as if to release the cobwebs of sleep and glanced at his sister.

"I do," he finally responded. "And it's a good thing as it appears I'll be needing a comfy chair in my sister's room for some time yet."

He was teasing. A part of her wanted to laugh. The grief of her friend's betrayal and tragic death jolted through her like a bolt of lightning, rubbing raw every tender corner of her being. All she wanted to do was cry. She thought the tears had dried up, but they hadn't. They flowed with renewed vengeance as the sorrow etched an aching hole deep inside.

"You feel hollow. Broken," Amell spoke softly with compassion. "I understand. But know this, Priya. She was not human. We managed to connect to her memory tapes and download a considerable amount of data before she self-destructed." He held up a hand to ward off protest. "And, yes, that's what she did. She self-destructed. When she couldn't win you over, she realized her mission was over. And the self-destruct mechanism activated."

Priya pondered her brother's words. Briefly. She used her sleeve to wipe away the last of the tears. Once her vision cleared, she glanced at him intently and asked, "What did you learn?" With a deep sigh of resignation, she sat back, leaning on her hands as she braced for his response.

"Like I said," Amell paused briefly to clear his throat. "She wasn't human. Some sort of advanced humanoid android. She could have fooled anyone, even a medical professional. That is, until she was cut open."

"If that's the case, how did you detect her robot qualities?"

"We have our own technology, Priya," her brother responded patiently. "In some ways, our technology is superior to theirs. In other ways, we have a long way to go. Like the tracker they put in the book. We might never have found it without your friend telling us where to look."

"But if she's an android, she's always under control from some exterior force. How and why would she direct us to the implant?" Priya had never been one to enjoy sci-fi flicks or books. She was a down-to-earth, feet firmly planted in reality type of person. But it didn't mean she was naïve about sci-fi technology and the endless realm of possibilities.

Amell was nodding his head in response. "We've considered that. Right now, we're searching through your entire collection of personal effects. You could help by giving us a list of anything Samantha gave you. And, Maurice, too, for that matter."

"Was he an android, too?" She had to know. How could she be fooled not once, but twice? Perhaps more often than she was aware.

"No. He was human. Programmed with implants. He's been dropped off on a deserted road near Bella Coola. We're tracking him as he wanders aimlessly. He doesn't remember anything before this moment. When he's picked up, he'll be registered at some medical facility as a John Doe."

"John Asshole Doe," Priya muttered under her breath.

Amell responded with a slightly raised eyebrow, then continued, "The list, Priya. We need it asap. What else did she give you?"

Instantly, Priya reached for her neckline, searching for the locket Maurice had presumably purchased for her while on one of their jaunts around Victoria. She rather liked the locket, holding onto it even though the two had disconnected, so to speak. It wasn't there.

"We thought of that." Amell noticed. "It's been analyzed. There was a tracking device inside."

"But I was with Maurice when he bought it," she argued.

Amell merely shrugged his shoulders. "Probably another planned exercise. Another operative."

"Is nowhere and no one safe and trustworthy?"

With a shake of his head, Amell responded, "Probably not. They have taken over far too much of this world."

"Will I get the locket back?" she asked tentatively. "I rather liked it, even if it was gifted to me by Maurice."

"I'm afraid not." Amell appeared remorseful. "It had to be destroyed. I can try to find you a replacement," he offered.

"Never mind." Priya waved away his offer. "I have others. Perhaps there was some sort of drug being released by the locket making me favor it so much. Now that it's gone, I don't seem to miss it. Not like I thought I would."

"You might be right about that," Amell agreed. "We still don't know all the technical abilities they possess."

"Everyone keeps talking about them and they. Who are they?"

"We don't know for sure," Amell admitted. "It's difficult enough keeping one step ahead of them. Right now, Priya, we need the list. Before they can send out more operatives and jeopardize all of Castle Mutasim."

"There was another book." Priya scrunched up her face, a habit from her youth when she was concentrating intently. "A first edition of Anna Sewell's *Black Beauty*."

Amell smiled at the memory. "Your first favorite book, as I recall. You made me read it every night until you knew it word for word by memory and you read it to me – or recited it."

"Read," Priya laughed at the shared recollection. She threw a pillow at her brother, another playful gesture from childhood. It missed, but he picked it up and threw it back, hitting her square in the face. "Hey!" she countered, throwing it harder this time and hitting the target.

"Children!" Kat scolded from the doorway. How long had she been standing there?

Priya giggled in response while Amell gave a sheepish look at his partner, hiding his discomfort with a nervous cough.

Amell is never nervous. Priya's lips stretched in a wide grin, her eyes sparkling. *Never.*

I do have that affect on him. Kat's voice countered in her head, making Priya grin broader.

"She's talking to you, isn't she?" Amell didn't wait for an answer. "Women!" he muttered. Turning to Kat, he said, "Another book. *Black Beauty.*"

"We found it," Kat assured them both. "Sensing Priya's love of books, and first editions at that, we did a thorough search of all the books she'd packed to bring here. The lab is analysing the implants as we speak. In a safe location underground. Then they will be destroyed and scattered near the labs in northern Alberta."

"Is that wise?" Amell cocked an eyebrow. "Going so close to Ground Zero, so to speak? Just to make a point?"

"And a point well made, I might add," Kat countered. "We can't live in fear, Amell. We can't allow them to intimidate us."

"Why not send me inside the lab?" Priya suggested. "I could scout things out. Then escape."

"No!" Amell bellowed pushing himself out of the chair, standing abruptly, stretching to his full height. "No! It's too dangerous, Priya. Once inside, we can't help you. No!" Noticing Kat's scolding glaze, he added, "At least, not yet. You're not ready." And he stormed out of the room, leaving the women shaking their head in mock disbelief.

"Men," they muttered in unison.

CHAPTER SEVENTEEN

"Are you okay?" A child's voice broke through her subconscious. She had been in a deep sleep. Again. "Are you okay?" The voice asked a little louder. Accompanied by a gentle tug on the arm. It was Amelie.

Priya forced her eyes open, squinting against the sudden splash of light. "Amelie. What are you doing here?" Her voice croaked. It was dry. She needed something to drink.

"Mother said you were unwell," the little girl responded. "I had to see if you were okay. I had to tell you that I've been practising."

"Practising?" Priya's mind was having trouble coming into focus.

"The piano," Amelie exclaimed, content to have her audience now fully awake. "I've practised everything you taught me. But I need you to teach me some more."

"Okay. I will. Soon."

"When?" The girl was insistent, but a knock on the door interrupted further discussion.

Wayne poked his head around the opening. "May I come in?" he asked timidly. Receiving no response, he took a tentative step across the threshold. His eyes fell on the little girl first. "Amelie," he exclaimed. "What are you doing here? Your mother is looking for you."

Amelie merely shrugged her shoulders and let out a shallow laugh. "Funny. Mother always knows where I am." She glanced back at Priya and gave her a warm smile. "I'll go back to my practising and see you later." And then she slipped out of the room as slick as a cat, or at least as slick as her mother. Wayne barely had time to step out of her way before she slithered past him.

"Off you go, Amelie," her father gave a firm command from just beyond the door.

"It would appear that my room is Grand Central Station," Priya croaked in a futile attempt at humor. It fell on deaf ears. Wayne was already in the room and her brother followed close behind.

"Any updates?" Amell asked, his question directed at Wayne.

He didn't answer Amell's question. Instead, focussing his attention on Priya, he asked, "Are you all right?"

Wayne stepped closer to the bed, allowing his eyes to hold Priya's with intensity. She felt a warmth flood through her as her once rescued mutt studied her closely.

She gave a slight nod of the head accompanied by a weak smile. "Yes, Wayne. I'm fine. It was a bit of a shock."

"I wanted to warn you about Samantha," Wayne spoke with conviction, firm, but quiet. "I knew she was a fraud, but I couldn't break my undercover image. I think she may have suspected me all along."

Raised eyebrows indicating surprise, Priya asked, "Then why didn't she say something?"

Wayne shrugged his shoulders. "Perhaps, robot or not, she had some deep feelings for you." Taking a deep breath, satisfied Priya was okay, for now, he focussed his attention on Amell. "We found three more miniscule implants. The crew continues to go through Priya's belongings." He paused to clear his throat. "The most recent find was in one of my dog toys that Priya had packed to bring along for her beloved mutt."

Amell bit his cheeks to stop a smile. Or, at least to attempt to. He failed. Priya didn't bother to contain her amusement, chuckling softly.

"And you never thought to sniff it out before?" Amell challenged. Priya couldn't tell if her brother was teasing Wayne, or asking with all seriousness. "Never mind." He waved off any answer. "It's been found now. It's all that matters." Glancing over

Wayne's shoulders, he spoke to Priya, "We'll leave you now. Come along, Wayne."

Amell left without another word, but Wayne held back. For so many months, he'd been Priya's constant companion. His resistance to Amell's suggestion spoke volumes of his feelings for the young woman.

"Amell's not accusing you, Wayne," Priya broke the silence, unfolding her legs and standing up. She walked toward the man who had once been her mutt. When she was close enough, she stopped and took his hands in hers. "It's not your fault."

"I know," Wayne responded in a soft voice, a muskiness in his tone sent shivers up and down Priya's spine. She couldn't help but lean in. Wayne pulled her in close and wrapped his arms around her, burying his face in the mussed hair at the top of her head. "I know. There was nothing to sniff," he muttered into her hair, the warmth of his breath sending more shivers along her spine. "They've created something that can't be sensed, with no noticeable aroma."

"Who are they?" Priya pushed back slightly, tilting her head to glance up into Wayne's face.

"I don't know, Priya. None of us do. Not really."

"Where are they, then?"

"There are labs all around the world. The closest one, the one where we believe we were all created, is in northern Alberta, just outside Cold Lake."

"In the oil sands?"

"Not quite, but close."

"I have to go there, Wayne," Priya admitted. "It's me they want. I have to go there and stop this. Somehow. Will you help me?"

Wayne stepped back, dropping his hands. He started pacing the room. "I can't, Priya," he shook his head to emphasize his point. "At least, not yet. We don't really know what we're up against. We have to have the means to extract you, and others who may choose to go along with you."

"I don't need extracting," Priya argued. "I can take care of myself."

He stopped, turning to face her, his face stern with conviction. "Not in this situation, you can't, Priya. It's not about sacrifice. If they capture you, there will no longer be a you. They will take over your body, your mind and so much more. Look what they did to Maurice. And Samantha was a mere robot. They have technology far advanced to anything we've ever encountered."

"But don't we have techno devices, too?" Priya countered his argument, determination fixed in her expression. "Aren't there some sort of mind blockers you can implant in me to protect me from their mind-controlling devices? Body shields? Anything?"

Wayne stood complacently, shaking his head, a look of dejection mirroring his response. "Just when we think we have something, Priya, they come up with something to counter it. They're always steps ahead of us. And," he held up his hands to ward off further protest, "just when we think we're learning their new techno tricks, they have invented something far more sophisticated. It's not a matter of losing you, Priya. It's a matter of survival for all of us. You are no longer just you. We are a unit here and we must work together for the good of everyone."

"So, what do we do?" she almost spat in disdain at being put in her place. "Just hide?"

"For now, yes," Wayne agreed. He resumed his pacing, allowing the silence to engulf the two and hopefully sooth some wounded emotions. When he came to a stop, he was standing in front of Priya once again. "Priya," he said, quietly. "You still have so much to learn here. And we have to visit Gwa'yasdams and learn from the first peoples."

"In the meantime, we hide and wait for their next assault?" she challenged. "They will come here, Wayne. They've found us. They've found Castle Mutasim."

Wayne shook his head slowly. "I don't think so, Priya. Amell has engineered a protective barrier, a dome of sorts. We're safe. For now."

"But you claim they're way ahead of us in techno knowledge," she argued, not willing to give up. Not yet.

"They are," Wayne agreed, letting out a deep sigh, and taking her hands in his. "But we have to trust in something. It's all we have. That and our ability to work together, to use our talents to protect and care for one another. That's one thing the human race could learn from us."

"Togetherness," Priya concluded.

"Yes, togetherness."

"One for all and all for one," she added the musketeer chant to lighten the mood.

"Indeed."

CHAPTER EIGHTEEN

Priya paced her room for the remainder of the afternoon. She pondered Wayne's words, Amell's concerns and Kat's gentle compassion. Part of her was drawn to the idea of storming the lab in northern Alberta. With all that had happened in the past few days, and it had only been a few days since she left Victoria, she was beginning to wonder how much of what she did and thought was her doing.

Who am I? she repeatedly asked herself as she paced. *Am I a lab rat? A pawn on someone else's chessboard? Do I, can I, even think for myself? What other implants have they installed in me that continue to remain undetected? Should I leave Castle Mutasim? Vanish in the night, just to keep everyone else here safe?*

No! She jumped. The voice inside her head was loud enough to erupt throughout her space. *No!* The voice repeated, imperative in its tone. It was Kat. Who else would have access to her mind? To her thoughts?

You are not a danger to anyone here at Castle Mutasim. The voice continued, content in the knowledge it had Priya's undivided attention. *You would be a greater danger out there. Beyond our protective barrier. They could and would find you and then you'd be forced to betray all you knew about us. About this place.*

No, I wouldn't, Priya argued back in her mind. *I wouldn't betray you. Or Amell. Or Wayne. Or the others.*

You would have no control over yourself, Priya. These are very powerful beings.

The voice vanished with a knock on the door. "May I come in?" It was Kat.

Priya chuckled, shaking her head. "I thought you already were."

Kat pushed the door ajar and slipped in quietly, like the cat-gene she possessed. "I don't intrude, Priya. Not unless compelled to do so. Something about your comments earlier and what Wayne shared of your conversation, I had to be sure. You're safer here. With us. We're all safer with you here."

Priya walked over to her bed and plopped herself down on the mattress with a huff. "Oh Kat!" she moaned. "I don't know what to think anymore. I don't even know what my thinking is and what is ingrained by some other high tech being. Are there still implants inside me? Controlling me?"

"It's quite possible," Kat agreed. "Amell asked me to come fetch you. Our techies want to run more tests on you. See if they've missed anything."

Priya groaned. "So, it's back to the dungeons."

"I'm afraid so. I don't like it any more than you do."

"I expected as much," Priya nodded somberly. Taking a deep breath, she stood up and pointed toward the door. "Lead the way, Kat. May as well get this done. I want to know, as much as the others, the danger I present to everyone here."

Kat led Priya down the grand staircase, then around to the rear of the castle, behind the conservatory and the library. It was a different route than the one Amell had taken earlier, not that Priya could remember it well. They came to what seemed to be a dead end, but Kat fiddled with a panel, and it swung open to reveal another set of stairs, leading downward.

"To the dungeons we go," Priya muttered with a feigned sense of humor. She had been there before. To see Samantha.

Kat merely responded with a "Watch your step. It's dark and the stairs are steep." Kat had no difficulty manoeuvring the passageway, her cat instincts allowing her to crawl, literally, up and down anything and everything. Priya, however, a mix of clumsy elephant, a brilliant creature of the waters and a dexterous creature which flew through the trees, found the deep, winding steps difficult and dizzying. The darkness, however, didn't bother her. She had superior eyesight in the dark. She would have thought the chimpanzee gene would have her swinging down the banister, but it didn't. Something she'd have to learn. It was a difficult descent, but she managed. With Kat in the lead to catch her if she stumbled, and hand firmly gripping the siderail, Priya took care with each step, letting out a deep sigh of relief when her foot touched solid ground.

"There's more," Kat informed her. "Another set of stairs. Steeper, too."

Priya groaned. Gripping the siderail again for support, she gingerly placed one foot in front of the other, descending one step at a time. This last series of steps went on infinitesimally. At least, it felt that way to Priya. It also spiraled in a tighter circle. It was like descending inside a dark tunnel. But there was some light from below, light at the end of the tunnel which grew brighter as the two descended further into the bowels of the earth beneath the castle.

The final step placed Priya on rather uneven footing. The floor was dirt-packed instead of the concrete or smooth wood surfaces she was accustomed to. The air felt heavier, too, but Priya's lungs adjusted, her dolphin genetics which would allow her to breathe underwater kicked in and made her breathing easier.

Kat wasn't so lucky. She was huffing in short breaths. "I don't venture down here often," she explained. "I can't take the thin air as well as you and Amell and others." She pointed straight ahead into the darkness beyond the small lighted area at the base of the stairs. "This way." As they walked forward, lights flickered on, marking the way, while further ahead appeared pitch black.

They made a few turns as one corridor after another lit up to mark their way. It was a maze of criss-crossing trajectories.

"I'm glad you know your way," Priya quipped.

Kat glanced back, tapping her nose. "My cat instincts," she proclaimed, and the ladies shared a chuckle. "The maze is another way to distract and confuse interlopers." Priya nodded in understanding.

Finally, they stopped. There was nowhere to turn, other than back the way they came and Priya doubted she could find her way out without assistance.

Priya glanced around nervously, studying the area immediately around them, the only section still lit so they could see. She noticed the walls were made of stone, stacked at random intervals and patterns. She reached out to touch one of the stones but stopped abruptly when Kat cleared her throat and shook her head.

Kat stood in the corner. She motioned Priya to come closer. Satisfied, Kat tapped on one wall to her right. Three times. She paused, then tapped on the wall to her left three times. She waited again. Raising both hands against the wall, she tapped short, long, short, long, short short, long short.

A voice boomed in response, "Enter."

"That's what I tapped in Morse code," Kat explained as the floor beneath their feet started to move in a circular pattern, transporting the two women through the wall, the grinding sound of stone against stone sending creaks and shivers up and down Priya's spine.

The space around them brightened as the sliding portal came to a stop. Priya blinked at the intensity of the light, following Kat's step off the platform with a bit of trepidation.

Amell greeted the two. "Priya," he said. "We have the machines ready. It's not much different than a CT scanner. More sophisticated in that it will pick up any transmissions emitting from inside the body and track the location. The procedure is pretty much the same. There is a change room in the corner," he motioned off to one end. "You need to disrobe and don one of the so-called hospital gowns and you will need to remove all your jewellery – anything metallic."

Priya gaped. Stunned. "Umm!" she muttered, taking a step back.

"It's okay, Priya," Kat reassured her in a calming voice. She had a hand on one of Priya's arms and the other in the gentle curve of her back. The touch and the voice soothed Priya and she allowed herself to be directed to the corner changing area.

The curtain was open. Kat pointed to the clean gown, neatly folded on the solitary chair. "Leave all your items on the chair. They have to be tested and cleansed thoroughly."

Priya stepped back again, putting pressure against Kat's restraining hold. "Is all this necessary? How do I know you're not them?" The realization of possible duping flushed through her mind as she spoke.

"You don't," Amell's voice, soft and composed, permeated from behind. "But there comes a time when we all have to trust someone, Priya. And I thought you trusted me."

Priya held back for a few more minutes. Calmly, she gave her head a slight nod and entered the changing space. She stood in the cramped area, listening as Kat whisked the curtains shut behind her. "I'll be right out here if you need me," Kat spoke in little more than a whisper. For Priya's ears only. Or had she spoken inside Priya's head. She was no longer sure.

Although small, there was room to manoeuvre. Barely. She slipped off the outer layers of her clothes, piling them neatly on the chair next to the gown. She tugged off her undergarments and placed them on top. Naked, she shivered, quickly shaking out the gown and slipping it over her shoulders. She tied the plastic sash around her waist, amazed at how such a short, flimsy length of plastic could stretch so far, with enough left over to tie securely. She wasn't wearing much jewellery; Amell had already taken the locket. Which left her watch, an old-fashioned analog clock face, the minute hand ticking steadily around the circumference, the hours clearly marked with numbers. As she unbuckled it, she glanced fondly at its face, gently winding the tiny nob, a habit from childhood, something she did every time she removed the watch. To keep it running. And it did keep running. It was a precious treasure. She thought back to the last Christmas with Amell. He had given her the watch and she had cared for it and worn it ever since.

"Know that I am with you whenever you wear this, Priya," he had said. *She thought his comment strange at the time, but she was too pleased with the gift to notice.*

"Are you ready?" Kat asked from beyond the curtained enclosure.

Priya didn't answer. She tugged open the drapes and marched out with determination. "Amell." she approached her brother. "Do you remember the last gift you gave me? As a child?"

Amell gave her a strange look. "Of course," he responded.

"What was it?"

"A watch."

Priya nodded. So far, the right answers, as she expected. "What did you say to me when you presented it?"

"Know that I am with you whenever you wear this," he quoted exactly.

Kat may have listened into her head as the memory resurfaced, but had she also transmitted the message to Amell so instantaneously?

"Are you testing me, Priya?" Amell asked. "Perhaps I should remind you what you said when you received it."

Priya crunched her brow, refusing her mind to bring up the memory, blocking out any intrusion. "What did I say, Amell?"

"Thank you, of course," he smiled knowingly, "followed by something to the effect of *I will wear it always and think of you forever.*"

"I did, didn't I?" she returned her brother's sigh, relief shadowing across her face.

"Is that sufficient to prove I am who I say I am?" Amell challenged. He knew her game. He knew her so well.

Priya merely shrugged. "The watch is in there." She nodded toward the changing area, "along with what little other jewels I wore. I have kept my promise to wear it always."

"That's good," Amell replied. "That's how we were able to track you and protect you all these years."

"It has an implant?"

Amell didn't answer. He didn't have to.

"Always looking out for me," she half whispered. "Or was it more like spying on me?"

Her brother grimaced. He'd heard, but he didn't respond. Clearing his throat with a loud rumble, as if trying to clear the air as well, he finished the rumbling with a cough and said, "Lie on the couch, Priya." He pointed to the CT scanner-like device which was already flashing lights in every direction. "Lie on your back with arms along your sides, palms down. The couch will slide into the bore of the gantry once you're ready and the lasers will do the rest. You must remain still. It's noisy. Just like a CT scanner. If you feel claustrophobic, close your eyes and count. If we do it right the first time, we shouldn't have to do it again."

Priya lay on the couch, as instructed. She didn't question Amell. He was in his all-business mode, something else she recalled from childhood. When Amell was 'all business', there was no distracting his attention to something or anything else.

Arms positioned at her sides, palms down, she closed her eyes and started counting. She had always been claustrophobic and the last thing she wanted to do was freak out whilst inside the bore and have to repeat the procedure. She felt the couch move; the air pressure thickened; the noise intensified; the entire contraption rattled with ferocious intent. She counted out loud, yelling the numbers as she winced her eyes shut. There was no way she was repeating this.

It seemed like forever, but it wasn't. The noise and the vibrations diminished, and the couch moved.

It's done, Kat's voice entered her head. Priya wasn't sure if it was subconsciously of consciously. The next words spoken were right next to her, as she felt a reassuring pat on the arm. "You may open your eyes, Priya. It's done."

Blinking, she realized she was lying underneath brilliant lights which scored deep pain as she winced to focus. Rolling to one slide, she half slid into a sitting position while her feet found traction on the floor. She was in a hurry to get off this thing. Too much in a hurry. Eyes still blinking, she stumbled to regain her balance, arms grappling her elbows to offer support.

"Breath deeply," Kat insisted. "Slowly. There now. You should be all right."

The grip on her arms eased and she stood on her own. Glancing around, her eyes came to rest on her brother, standing to one side, close enough to offer assistance if needed. "Anything?" she asked simply. "Did you find anything?"

"Several," he answered. "They've been disabled and will have to be removed."

"Now?"

"The sooner, the better," Amell insisted. "They may have means to reactivate the devices. We can't take any chances."

CHAPTER NINETEEN

Once again, Priya woke up in the bed in her room. At least, it's how she recognized it now. It was hers. For the time being. Perhaps forever.

She blinked her eyes trying to force them open, force them to stay focused. "Don't rush it," Kat's voice came from across the room.

Priya shifted her head in the general direction and noticed Kat sitting in the same seat by the hearth which Amell had claimed the first time she woke up in this bed, in this room. The room around her spun at the slight head movement. She blinked again. Several times. The spinning settled.

"Kat," she croaked. Her voice felt like sandpaper. Kat stood up and walked over to the bed. She reached for something on the side table and Priya heard what sounded like water being poured into a glass.

Gently lifting the girl's head, Kat held the cup to Priya's lips. "Drink," she insisted. "Slowly."

Priya took several gulps before turning away, shaking her head slightly. It was refreshing, but she couldn't swallow any more water. Not yet. She cleared her throat. Kat lowered Priya's head to the pillow and replaced the cup, before perching herself on the side of the bed. "How do you feel?" she asked.

"Like I've just awoken from a bad dream," Priya croaked. The sips of water hadn't improved the quality of her voice and her mouth still felt like sandpaper. "Did they get them all?" She glanced at Kat.

"We think so." the cat-blended human nodded slightly. "Amell wants to do another scan to be sure. But not today. He wants you to rest first. You had a rough time. They had to go deep into your skull. Into the cerebellum, next to the brain stem. As well as deep within the somatomotor cortex and the somatosensory cortex."

Priya blinked. Tried to clear her brain. Her thoughts. "The what?" she asked. Confusion cushioned like a suffocating blanket; her head spun without compulsion.

Kat patted Priya's hand gently. "Never mind. Suffice it to say, it was not an easy extraction. We're just relieved to have the implants out and you safely back among us."

"So, you've been allocated the task of watching over me."

"In a manner of speaking. We also figured you'd have a multitude of questions when you woke up and, since I appear to be the most patient of our lot," she paused to allow her words to sink in. "Probably the cat gene in me," she added with a twinkle of humor reflected in her eyes. "They assigned me the task. The others are out on patrol, either along the castle battlements or beyond. We're never safe, Priya. Never."

"And I brought danger to your doorstep," Priya bemoaned. "It's all my fault."

"No, Priya." Kat took the young woman's hand in hers. "No. It's no one's fault except those who created us. Those who hunt us down like wild beasts."

Priya closed her eyes for a minute, pondering Kat's words. When she reopened them, she asked the question which first popped into her head when she discovered Kat and her brother were a couple. "How did you meet?" She noticed Kat's surprise before the cat-human banked it down. "You and Amell. How did you meet? I want to hear it all. The entire love story." She quirked a half grin as she allowed her fingers to air quote the last part. "I know my brother would never tell. But I hope you will."

Kat shook her head, laughing gently. "Not much to tell."

Priya wasn't fooled. The sparkle in Kat's eyes betrayed her true feelings. "That's what they all say. Now spill. He is my brother, after all. I have to know the deets. Besides, it'll help me relax."

"Deets," Kat let out a deep, rumbling purr, another one of her cat-ish quirks. "You young people do enjoy destroying the English language."

"You're procrastinating, Kat." Priya playfully nudged Kat with her knee.

"Very well," Kat relented with a huff. "But I'm warning you. It's quite simple. We met. We fell in love. We became a couple."

"And you had children together," Priya added. "But I want the deets, Kat. Not the outline."

"Shall I change form and curl up next to you, purring while I share the entire tale?" she asked with a coy look on her face.

"You can do that?"

"Of course," she exclaimed, slapping her palms on her lap, pinching her eyes tight, and curling into a ball. With a short meow, Kat transformed into a tabby cat, soft and cuddly. "What do you think?"

"Wow!" Priya was amazed. "Can everyone do this? I mean change into their alternate genetic makeup?"

"Most can," Kat replied. "Some are still learning. Wayne is perhaps the best changer in our group. You only knew him as a mutt until you arrived here."

"True. Very true." She reached out and ran a hand along Kat's back. She purred in response and Priya jumped, pulling her hand back. "I'm sorry. I shouldn't have done that."

"Why?"

"I don't want to offend you."

"Never mind that. It felt good." Kat purred again, blinking her eyes enticingly.

"I have to ask." Priya paused in the petting. "What happened to your clothes? I mean when you changed to cat form?"

Kat chuckled softly, a sound which sounded more like a purr. "I'm still wearing clothes, Priya. It's part of the changing magic. Of what they did to us." She shuddered and resumed human form. Fully clothed.

"Wow!"

Curling into a ball again, Kat reclaimed her cat form and snuggled in for more attention. "Dig your fingers deeper into my coat and you'll feel the fabric of my clothes."

Priya did as instructed. Feeling around, she felt the tense fabric, which could either be the cat's skin or clothing. It was difficult to tell. "It's my clothes," Kat reassured her. "I'm never naked in my changing forms. You can be rest assured of that."

Priya couldn't resist a soft giggle as she continued to run her hand along Kat's back again. "Back to my question about you and Amell," she insisted. "Now that we're both comfortable, spill it. All of it."

"Why don't you ask your brother?" Kat delayed further by asking her own question.

"You really think he'd tell me?" Priya chuckled. "He is male, after all."

"True enough." Kat purred some more, shimmying a little closer to Priya's hand. "Very well. Here goes. We met at the lab. While I talk, you may rub my back. It feels good." Priya obliged and the two settled in for a gab. "I guess you could say, each one of us has a story that began in the lab. Your brother, Amell, after he left you, he barely kept ahead of them as they continued to track him down. He connected with Roderick--you've met him." Priya nodded her head as Kat continued, "Roderick helped Amell, keeping him ahead of the trackers. Roderick had already begun a network of mutants like us and he was planning a rescue mission at the lab north of Edmonton. Amell jumped right in. But he was also able to help in other ways. You know Amell has a brilliant mind; he's a whiz with numbers." Priya nodded again. "Well, he started playing the markets and brought in a considerable amount of money to furnish the rescue mission and, eventually, to purchase this land and build the castle. He still plays the markets and makes a bundle, more than enough to keep us well fed, safe and as up-to-date as possible on high tech and tracking devices."

Kat paused and lavished in Priya's attention, snuggling in even closer than before. If it was possible. "Well, the night he arrived at the lab, I was being tested for what, I don't know. They were always running tests on us. This one was quite painful. I must have been screaming up a storm, because I drew the rescue team's attention to my location. Amell was the first to barge into the lab where they were doing the tests. I didn't take much notice at first, as there were all manner of mutants in the facility; some were allowed free access to move around, while others, like myself, were kept locked in cages. But Amell – his temper knew no bounds. When he saw the pain they were inflicting on us, me in particular, he went berserk. He trashed the lab and killed everyone working within, even one of the mutants who had been programmed to protect and defend. The alarms were blaring all over the facility; people, creatures were running helter-skelter. Amell didn't stop until he had unbound the straps and picked me up in his arms. As he walked by various cages, he unleashed more fury, kicking them open and freeing the inhabitants."

"Wouldn't the locks be secure, coded?" Priya interrupted.

"You would think," Kat purred her response. "But they were too confident in their sense of indestructibility. They didn't see the need to install anything more secure than a padlock. The entire facility was well secure, but not the cages within." She paused, allowing Priya's strokes to sooth her. "Now. Where was I? Oh yes. All the mutants in the cages escaped and followed Amell, who was still carrying me tenderly in his arms. They followed us to the nearest exit, which Amell kicked open, his anger still brewing to a boiling point. We were well beyond the facility before the pain that had been inflicted eased enough that I could take notice of my rescuer. Oh my! And I was smitten right away.   He was quite my dashing knight in shining armor who had come to the rescue. Moreso." She let out a deep sigh. "And the rest is history." She cleared her throat, gave her body a shake, stood up and stretched. She transformed to the human counterpart; the Kat Priya had first met.

"I'm sure there's more," Priya chuckled.

"Perhaps," Kat smiled coyly. "But that's all you're getting. Amell and his recruits, for he was now the leader, along with Roderick and those he rescued, made haste to Vancouver Island where Amell had purchased this property and we all worked together to build our safe place. Our refuge."

"Castle Mutasim."

"Exactly!" Standing up, Kat reached out a hand to her new friend, her sister-in-law. "Now, don't you go getting any ideas about breaking into a lab on your own. Amell had an entire team of mutants, all with a task to complete. And, even with the number of rescuers, they didn't all make it out alive. We lost some. It's a suicide mission, Priya. If anyone in our team feels threatened for re-capture, they are to self-destruct, in an explosive way to leave behind as much damage as possible. It's not a walk-in-the-front-door and expect a pleasant welcoming committee. Not with these people. You need training and you must be ready, heart, mind and soul. When you're ready, when Amell feels you're ready, you'll be included in one of our rescue missions. Understood?"

"Wayne talked to you?" Priya answered with a simple question.

"He didn't have to, Priya." Kat continued to hold out her hand.

With a nod of understanding, Priya grasped it. As long as she was allowed to confront 'them' at some point, she would wait. And train. "Understood," she gave a reluctant consent.

"Now. Let's go get something to eat. I'm starving."

Priya responded to Kat's gentle tug, standing up slowly, allowing the blood to circulate through her limbs. A growl rumbled from deep within her stomach. The two women chuckled. "I guess I am, too," she admitted.

CHAPTER TWENTY

Priya hadn't realized how little she knew. About anything. She discovered a completely different side of her brother she never knew: relentless drill sergeant being the worst. She was taxed to the extreme on every aspect of her gene pool. The castle included an Olympic sized swimming pool and Priya's morning regimen began with a vigorous hour in the pool. Under normal circumstances, if there were such a thing, she would love the time in the pool. This, however, was work – endurance testing to the extreme.

Priya's dolphin gene included more than the aquatic mammal's high intelligence. The dolphin could swim and dance both in and above the water. Priya was required to do lengths in the pool, at surface level and below water, extending her ability to survive for longer periods of time while submerged in water, or, should the situation arise, in an environment devoid of oxygen. She was given aqua-aerobic workouts, dancing at the water's surface, like a synchronized swimmer. She was exhausted when she hauled herself out of the water to retreat to the showers.

The day didn't end there. After an extensive breakfast, and she was eating a lot more than her usual intake, she was subjected to hours of further study in the library. Amell was filling her mind with facts, not just on the lab rats they all were, but specifically on the various mammals whose genes she possessed.

Before lunch, she joined many of the others in a jog around the upper ramparts, partly to observe the goings-on beyond the fortifications, but also to build their stamina.

"You never know when you'll need to run like the wind," Amell explained, "charge like an elephant or swim like a dolphin."

After lunch, another big feast, it was back to the research, before her final workout of the day: swinging through the trees. At least, it's how Priya thought of it. Her chimpanzee genes, she quipped, only in her mind, but loud enough for Kat to chuckle along. She spent time on the trampoline, climbing ropes and other apparatus and, yes, quite literally, swinging through the air, at least, if not through the trees.

By supper, she was starved, aching and ready to crash for the night. Which was not to be. Not right away, anyway.

"You have one more gene you didn't know about," Amell explained. "In fact, we only just discovered it when we did a more thorough test of your bloodwork. You have the owl gene."

She was stunned. "I suppose that explains my perfect night vision," she responded. "But I can't fly."

"You will," Amell insisted. "Sissy, here, is going to teach you to fly."

Sissy, the mutant bald eagle/ human, was the castle's main source of intel from the outside world. She spent a good portion of her waking hours, day and night, scouring through the clouds, swooping down through the trees and sending images back to the castle communications network. She had an implant, a camera of sorts, one she had suggested installing in one of her eyes. Priya had cringed when Sissy described it. The mere thought of something implanted into one's eye sent shivers up and down Priya's spine. It was a useful implant, however, one which benefited the entire castle and its residents. It was the camera implant which had tracked Priya's so-called friends, leading to their capture.

The first flying lesson was a disaster. Sissy was good at what she did, but her talents obviously didn't include teaching.

"Like this," she explained to Priya as the two stood on the ramparts looking over the forested land beyond the castle. Sissy spread her wings and jumped, or so it appeared. She swooped down, through the trees, did a circle and returned to the ramparts, landing with the elegance of a ballerina, in the same spot she had left only moments before. "Now you try," she instructed, with a smile which gave the impression of being encouraging.

It wasn't. "Small problem," Priya pointed out. "I don't have any wings."

"Oh!" Sissy stepped back. "Right. Amell," she yelled over her shoulder. "No wings. How's she supposed to fly?"

"Spread the arms and jump," Amell called back. "Fly close and catch her if she falls, but the wings should appear as the air rushes beneath her outspread arms."

"Yeah. Right." Priya wasn't so sure. In spite of her mixed genes which facilitate swinging through trees and the new owl gene she recently discovered, she wasn't all that confident her wings would miraculously appear should she decide to jump.

Sissy shrugged. "It worked for me," she said. "I'd forgotten about that. My first flight was like yours. I jumped with arms spread wide and all of a sudden, I was flying. Wings and all."

Priya remained unconvinced. Amell and Kat moved in closer and added their words of encouragement. "You can do it," Amell spoke in his calm, soothing voice. Kat echoed his words, speaking in Priya's head.

She stepped back from the brink. She couldn't do it. Swinging through trees was one thing, but this? No way! "No!" Priya shook her head vehemently to emphasize her stand. She took another step back, reaching the inner boundary of the rampart. Another step and her foot met with a void. Amell rushed to catch her, but he wasn't quick enough. Priya teetered and tumbled backward into the courtyard. Her scream shook the castle walls, but she felt nothing. Saw nothing. Considering her eyes were glued shut, it was no wonder. Everything was black. Until.

She didn't crash land, that's for sure. Falling backward didn't help project the wings, especially since they were reaching upward as she fell backward. It wasn't a pretty sight. She was caught, by a whooshing of wings and claws grasping her torso.

Birds of all shapes and sizes had come to the rescue, in the process of stemming her fall, they had managed to flip her over, expand her arms on either side and support her body until she was airborne, soaring high in the sky. And, yes, finally, with wings. When she opened her eyes, she was weaving and floating above the trees, over the castle, swooping and diving like a winged pro.

"I'm flying," she shrieked. No one heard her. Except Kat. "I'm flying!"

Yes, you are, Kat spoke inside her head. *You really are flying. Care to return to the nest? Your brother is worried you might go too far.*

Let him worry, Priya retaliated. *It's his fault I'm in this mess.*

Kat chuckled in response.

She did return. Not long after. Her wings, unused to the strain, were tiring. She landed with the prowess of a seasoned flyer. Wrapping her wings around her front, the silky, dark feathers which stretched the length of her arms, vanished as her hands, which had never disappeared in the transformation, clasped together with satisfaction. She was hooked. Fear aside, now, she loved it.

CHAPTER TWENTY-ONE

"Time for a break," Wayne announced the following morning as breakfast concluded. Priya was heading out for more training, but her erstwhile friend stopped her. "It's time to visit Gwa'yasdams, don't you think?" The question wasn't just aimed at Priya, but to the others as well who hovered nearby.

"I want to come, too," Amelie, forever Priya's shadow, spoke with giddy reverence. "Can I come, Priya? Can I?"

"Me, too," George, never one to be left out, quickly added his voice. "I want to go, too. Are you going in the stealth copter? That is so cool. Can I sit up front?"

The children were chattering freely, not concerned their request might be denied. It was unthinkable. They were game for the adventure and convinced they'd be allowed to come along for the ride.

Amell cleared his throat. "Children," he used his stern, fatherly voice, the one Priya remembered so well from her childhood. She had to hide a smile as the memories surfaced. "You have classes today. This outing is for Priya alone."

"But Wayne's going," George argued. His face was forming into a pout. He didn't like the idea of being left behind. "And I bet Roderick is going to pilot the copter."

"Yes and yes," Amell nodded his head. "You are quite right, George. However, you will recall there are only four seats in the copter and three have already been claimed. I'm not about to choose between you and your sister."

"We could share the remaining seat," Amelie suggested. She didn't want to be left behind either.

"Not safe," Amell pointed out. "Besides, as I pointed out, this outing is primarily for Priya. Not you two. Now, I do believe your teacher is waiting for you. Upstairs. Right?"

The nodding heads was a glum sight. George turned and trudged off. Amelie held back, hoping they'd change their minds. They didn't.

"Amelie," Amell spoke softly, but with a firm tone which allowed no room for argument.

"Yes, Father." With a deep sigh, she embraced her aunt in a warm hug before reluctantly following her brother upstairs.

Turning to the others, Amell said, "I think this is a good idea. Things have been quiet enough and Priya is prepared for just about anything. It should be safe. As George suggested, Roderick will fly you over in the copter." He glanced at Roderick who nodded in agreement.

"Why don't I use my own wings?" Priya suggested.

"Not in broad daylight," Amell scolded gently. "Not where people will see you and ask questions. This is better."

"Besides," Wayne added, "you must be exhausted from all the training. And you've never attempted to carry someone while you flew."

"Always a first time," she muttered, but she reluctantly agreed. No point in attracting unwanted attention from the outside world. Turning to Roderick, she asked, "You don't mind?"

"Not at all," he gave her a warm smile. "I haven't been to Gwa'yasdams in some time. And," he quickly added with a side glance to Amell, "we all need a break from training and the castle from time to time."

Amell merely grunted.

"I'll meet you at the copter pad on the roof in ten minutes," Roderick announced.

"Sounds good," Priya agreed. She noticed Wayne's hesitation and wondered at his disgruntled look. Didn't he want Roderick to fly them over? Was he feeling a pang or two of jealousy? Or, was it something else? She shrugged it off. She liked both Wayne and Roderick and now she could enjoy a day with the two of them, away from the expectations at the castle.

When Priya joined her travel companions on the castle roof, they were arguing about something. They stopped abruptly when she was within earshot. "Anything wrong?" she asked, trying to discern which one had the more guilty look. They both did. She shrugged. "Okay, then. Let's go. I'm ready."

"Wayne, climb into the back," Roderick ordered gruffly. "Priya, you sit up front next to me. That way you'll have the best view." His tone of voice offered no room for argument.

Priya climbed in and fastened her seatbelt while the men took their places doing the same. She watched as Roderick fiddled with various controls and the copter suddenly lifted vertically. "Soundless?" she queried.

"Like George said, this is our stealth copter," Roderick explained. He didn't have to yell as one would expect sitting in a noisy copter. It ran sleek and quiet as the newest high-speed commuter train. The only indication it was actually running was the rising altitude and a slight vibration which felt more like a gentle massage than anything else.

"Impressive." Priya nodded her approval.

"Better to slip in and out of places unnoticed," Wayne commented from the rear.

"I'd say," Priya agreed. "How long's the flight?"

"About forty minutes," Roderick replied, guiding the copter in a general easterly direction. They flew above the tops of trees which had grown on Vancouver Island for almost a century, perhaps longer. When she noticed a strip of water on the horizon, Roderick explained they were approaching the coast. "We're over the island coast just north of Comox Island. You can see the totem poles at Alert Bay to your left. Then we'll fly across the islands dotting the Johnstone Strait until we reach Health Bay on Gilford Island.

Some people call it Health Lagoon. The small community of Gwa'yasdams is on the west side of the island near Health Bay."

"Are there people still living there?"

"Yes. A few. Not sure of the numbers." Roderick eased the copter, banking more to the right, coasting over narrow water passageways dotted with islands of all shapes and sizes. Many had narrow beaches, bordered by lush, thick forests, untouched by loggers.

Priya let out a gasp. "It's beautiful. So peaceful."

"Prime real estate for the First Nations way back in the day when they needed safe harbors near good fishing grounds." Roderick was doing all the talking. Wayne was sitting back in his seat, arms crossed, and, when Priya glanced back, she noticed a scowl, which he quickly replaced with a smile when he noticed her looking at him.

"There were a lot of fabulous totem poles and decorated longhouses, back in the day. When Emily Carr visited in 1912, she listened to stories from the Elders about the Wild Woman of the woods."

"D'Sonoqua."

"Yes. D'Sonoqua."

"Like the wicked witch in Hansel and Gretel," Priya added. "A story to frighten children so they wouldn't wander off alone into the woods."

"Exactly. They erected totem poles of D'Sonoqua to remind people of all ages of the dangers in the forests. Danger everywhere, really."

"But, was she real? Was D'Sonoqua real?"

"It's what we believe. Now that we know all about the mutant projects and how far back in history they existed, we believe D'Sonoqua was one of these creations." Roderick was circling a bald patch near the beach of one of the larger islands. "Gilford Island," he explained. "This is where we'll set down. Away from the community. Our stealth mode will allow us to land undetected.

Unless someone is out on their fishing vessel nearby. But I don't see anyone. So, we should be clear to slip in unnoticed."

"Why stealth and secrecy?" Priya was a little concerned with the increased need for obscurity. "Why can't we just walk in and pretend to be tourists?"

"They don't care much for tourists," Roderick answered bluntly. "We represent those who came and stole their lives, their land and their pride. And so much more. Better to visit unobserved."

As the copter set down, Priya unfastened the seatbelt and prepared to step out. "We'll stay together," Roderick advised. "I'll take the lead."

"Of course," Wayne grumbled from the rear. He climbed out after Priya and gently took her arm, leading her toward the treeline. He whispered into her ear. "He was always a bit of a control freak."

"I can hear you," Roderick called from behind.

Priya glanced over her shoulder and gasped. "The copter. Where is it?"

"Camouflaged. Another great Amell invention." Roderick stepped ahead of the pair and marched into the woods. "We can talk as we walk."

And Priya wanted to talk. She still had a lot of unanswered questions. "Is D'Sonoqua still around?"

"We believe she is."

Wayne cut in. "She hasn't been seen for decades and then, all of sudden, there have been numerous sightings."

"The same D'Sonoqua?" Priya asked, glancing from one to the other of her escorts.

"We're not sure," Roderick answered. "None of us have encountered her. Yet."

"Perhaps we will today," Wayne suggested, letting out a muffled growl. "I'm ready. Are you?"

Roderick merely shook his head and marched ever forward into the thicker part of the forest. "This way."

"Has this new D'Sonoqua stolen children? Or merely scared people?"

"The latter," Wayne muttered a brief response. "People, those who are pure human, scare far too easily."

Priya sheltered a glance at the one who had been her stalwart companion for so long. She was beginning to realize she really didn't know him. Or anyone else for that matter. This was a disgruntled, unhappy side of Wayne she'd never before witnessed.

The group trudged deeper into the forest. The trees were vast, thick trunked and tall, sheltering the group from the clear sky above and the rays emitted by the mid-afternoon sun. It was dark, but not too dark to see. And, Priya was learning to appreciate her owl genes with the empowered night vision.

"Where are we headed?" she asked to neither of her companions in particular. "Aren't we going to the community? To Gwa'yasdams?"

"Not the current community," Roderick explained, not missing a step in his march. "To the old village."

"It still stands?" Priya was aghast. "It must be well over a hundred years old. How?"

"It stands. Barely." Roderick paused briefly, pointing straight ahead. A whiff of salt water breeze filtered through the trees. They were approaching another beach, what once must have been the landing site for countless Kwakwaka'wakw, local fishermen and visiting tribes. Priya wanted to stop, to soak it all in. She was treading on ancient lands. Breathing deeply, she closed her eyes, pondering the sanctity of the space around her.

Roderick nudged her and continued his march, talking as they broke a path through to the beach. "The D'Sonoqua totem I wish to show you toppled over fifty or more years ago. It lies in the thick forest regrowth, being consumed by nature. But there is enough of it remaining to allow you to appreciate the creature and the art it inspired."

A high-pitched shriek pierced through the air, making Priya jump. The others glanced around, equally startled. "What was that?" she asked.

"D'Sonoqua, I suspect," Wayne answered, his voice not as surly or as intense as it had been.

Roderick merely picked up his pace, as if approaching the beach and leaving behind the forest would offer them more protection. If protection was what they needed. The shriek repeated. Closer. Priya stumbled over some fallen branches, falling to her knees.

Wayne shouted. "Change, Priya. Change." He and Roderick had already switched to their dominant mutant forms, Wayne the dog and Roderick the fox. They scattered into the woods, hunting or avoiding the hunt, Priya didn't know which, while she scrambled to her feet.

"Wait!" she called out in vain, but it was too late. Her escorts had vanished. She was alone. In the forest. With a strange creature trekking ever closer. She could hear the crunching of underbrush. Was it Roderick? Wayne? Or the unknown? D'Sonoqua? "Wait!" She stood frozen in place. Unable to move. Her weeks of training useless, for here, in the moment of urgency, she couldn't think of what to do. Mind freeze! Lifting her head slowly, she let out a wail of frustration, the volume of her voice matching the creature in pursuit. The crashing was mere feet away and yet, still, she saw nothing but the forest. The trees. The shrubs. The annoying vines and fallen branches which threatened, and did, trip her. Again.

And, finally, she knew what to do. She ran. There wasn't room enough to spread her wings and fly. At least, she didn't think so. Jumping to the lowest tree branch, she used her chimpanzee prowess to grab hold and swing. She gained momentum in the swaying motion and swung herself to the next branch. A little higher this time. A little lower the next. Until she found herself facing a long stretch of sand and gravel and the wide, open waters beyond.

The beach. They had been headed toward the beach. The ancient village had stood along this stretch. Nothing remained. Only sand. Gravel. And the flapping waves lapping against the shoreline.

She swung once more and landed in a thick, soft patch of sand. The crunching was still close. Behind her. All around her. It echoed in the open spaces. Was this a test? Had Roderick and Wayne been set up to abandon her here? To test her abilities? She didn't have time to ponder the possibility. An ear-piercing shriek, mere feet behind, made her jump and set off in a burst of momentum. She ran toward the water and splashed in the incoming tide, leaving a sloshing sound in her wake as she plundered ever forward.

But the creature, whatever it was, continued its pursuit. She was the prize. The victim. And, before the beach ended, she felt something grab her firmly, swinging her body in a circular motion as a parent might spin a child for pleasure. Only this wasn't pleasure. And she was being swung much higher, much faster, until with a single toss she landed wrapped around a furry set of shoulders, hands and feet firmly gripped. She tried to resist. No use. The grip was too tight. She tried to scream, but only earned a mouthful of rancid, fowl-smelling fur which made her gag.

The creature roared. Shrieked. Roared some more. And ran. The motion was jolting. Jarring. Priya bounced relentlessly, her body repeatedly bruised with each new contact it made with the creature as the two plunged back into the forest. As branches chortled against the two, Priya sought refuge by burying her head in the furry shoulder, breathing gently so as not to gag further at the stench. It was either that or have her head scraped to shreds by resisting tree appendages.

They tore deeper into the forest, up and down inclines until finally the creature stopped. Abruptly. Dropping Priya roughly to the ground.

Winded and sore, she forced herself to sit, pulling her legs toward her chest and taking the opportunity to glance around the setting. She had landed on a bare sheet of rock, a cleared patch surrounded by thick overgrowth and dense forest. She had no idea where she was or what was happening. There was enough space to spread her arms, to make them into wings and fly away. But where? And, just as the thought entered, it was dashed as the creature began tying something around Priya's body, preventing her from spreading the wings.

"To keep you here," it spoke.

Priya, startled, used her heels to push her body back. Away. As far as she could.

"No way out," it spoke again. "You stay with me." It grunted and sat down in the limited space remaining, taking up every inch with its massive body.

Priya gasped as her eyes came to rest on the creature's after doing a cursory glance at its entirety. The body was a massive extension of fur. It was unclothed, no need with the layers of furs. The chest, however, indicated it was female. But the eyes! They were intense. Dark. Brooding and caring, all in one. And clever. There was a depth of intelligence Priya hadn't expected in such a creature.

"Like what you see?" It broke the silence again, the lips spreading wide, baring badly yellowed long teeth, the incisors sharply pointed. "Now that you've finished studying me, I'd like to point out there's no way off this cliff. And no way up it. Your arms are tied to your body to prevent you from taking flight." She waved a hand to ward off commentary. "Oh yes! I know all about you. I know what you can do. I know what they can do, too." She waved her arms again for emphasis. "And don't think for a minute with all their super-mutant abilities they can find you or reach you here.

You're with me. You're safe. From them. And from me. I will not harm you. I just want to talk."

"How? Why?" Priya gasped, banking down the mounting terror within. As best she could. "And who are you?"

The creature sat, cross-legged, folding its massive body into a tight bundle. Facing Priya, it maintained its lips in a wide arch in what might be interpreted as a grin. Certainly not friendly enough to be a smile.

"They call me D'Sonoqua," it said. "Wild woman, others say. I am not wild. I am only different. As are you. We were created in the same lab."

CHAPTER TWENTY-TWO

The voice was clear. Concise. Articulate. Priya continued to study the creature. "Do you have a name?" she finally asked. "Something other than what they call you?"

It gave a grin-like expression. Again. "Susan. I always liked the name Susan. Call me Susan."

"But it's not your name, is it?" The creature shook her head. "All right, I'll call you Susan. And I'm Priya."

"I know who you are." Susan shifted her head to spit into the dirt away from the two. "We were created in the same lab. At the same time. With the same parent genes. The same mother and father. We're sisters."

Priya's eyes bulged in surprise. "Sisters? But, you've been here for centuries."

"Others. Not me. We're Sasquatch."

"Big Foot."

"Another bad name and all because we have big feet." And, to emphasize the point, she stretched out her legs so Priya could examine them.

"Yes, I see. They definitely are big." She studied the feet briefly, before returning her gaze to Susan's face. "How many are there? How many Sasquatch?"

Susan shrugged her shoulders. "Many. Like you and the others. We were created in a lab. Mutated. Abused. Tested. Prodded. Educated. Programmed. And many of us escaped. Some were captured and reformed within the lab facilities. Others, like me, managed to remove all tracking devices and remain hidden. Safe. For now. But it's no longer safe. You have brought one of them here. He is not to be trusted."

"Who? Roderick? Wayne?"

The creature merely shrugged again. "Unknown. I just know one is dangerous. Right now, they both seek your attentions. But something sinister dwells within." She waved a hand, brushing away a swarm of flies.

"How do you know this?" More questions. "How do you know Roderick or Wayne or both are dangerous?"

"I have my ways." She shrugged again. It appeared to be a nervous tick: shrugging. "Part of my genetic mutation included some sort of an extra-sensory perception ability. Humans, those pure, call it ESP for short. Some use it to read people's future." Another shrug. It was definitely an auto-reflex movement of some kind or other.

"So, you sense either Roderick or Wayne is dangerous," Priya pondered aloud. "But you don't know which one?" She studied her captor. Noticing a twitch in the eye, followed by the now familiar shoulder shrug, she added, "You know, don't you? Then tell me."

"Amell knows. You will, too, when the time is right. You probably wouldn't believe me if I told you now. Best you find out on your own terms."

Priya glared at Susan, trying to make sense of her opponent. Sister? Family? Could she be? "How long have you been here? And why do you stay here?" It was Priya's turn to wave her hand, absently brushing away the pesky bugs.

A sneeze startled the two. Susan jumped up and prowled the confined space. "Who goes there? Come out or I'll sniff you out and worse."

A whimper. "It's just me."

"Amelie." Priya tried to stand, but her restraints held her back.

"Amell's daughter?" Susan asked. "What's she doing here?"

"You mean you couldn't sense her?" Priya asked, astonished.

Susan crouched down on all fours and peered over the edge. "There you are." She reached out one arm. "Grab hold and I'll pull you up. Then you have some explaining to do. Especially how you've managed to avoid my ability to detect."

As Amelie was lifted from the cliff-clinging branch where she was perched, she couldn't help but ask her questions. "Is she really my aunt?" She had obviously been listening for some time.

"How much did you hear?" Priya asked. "And how did you get here? You were on the way to the schoolroom when I last saw you."

Amelie smiled coyly and settled on the rock slab, closer to Priya than the creature she now knew as her aunt. "Two aunts. I'm so lucky." She beamed, expertly avoiding the questions.

"Amelie," Priya scolded. "You have some explaining to do."

With a deep sigh, she cast a wary glance to Priya, then to Susan and back to Priya again.

"You have to 'fess up," Susan insisted, plopping herself back down at the opposite end of the confining platform.

"Why is Aunt Priya tied up?" She was quite the negotiator. Amelie managed a glare at her newly discovered aunt. "She's no danger to you. And she has just as many questions as I do. So, we're not leaving here till we have our answers." She nodded toward Priya. "So. Untie her."

"Demanding little one, isn't she?" Susan chuckled, but she moved from her perch and reached across to untie the binds holding Priya in place. "There. Go, if you must. Or stay for more answers."

"First. Amelie, you have some questions to answer."

Another deep sigh. "Oh, very well," she began with a forced huff. "Mother and Father don't know what I can do. I've only just found out myself."

"What can you do?" Priya and Susan asked in unison, Priya stifling a gasp when she realized this sister creature had mimicked her without prepping.

"I can make myself invisible," Amelie admitted. To prove her point, she scrunched her eyes shut and the next minute, she wasn't there.

"What?" Susan exclaimed. "Where did she go?"

"I'm right here, Aunt Susan," the girl answered and right away appeared sitting as she had been before she vanished.

"Wow! But how?" Priya asked.

She was rewarded with a shoulder shrug. Must be a family thing, this shoulder shrugging. "I don't know, Aunt Priya. George was teasing me a few weeks before you arrived. I was so mad. I scrunched my eyes and then I heard him yell, *where are you?* I hadn't realized I'd vanished. We tried it a few more times and it worked every time. I think he was jealous, but we both agreed it would be more advantageous if we kept it a secret between us. That way we could snoop on the goings-on at the castle."

"Amelie," Priya scolded lightly. "You know it's not polite to snoop and eavesdrop."

"I know." The girl shrugged again. "But there's so much going on that we don't understand. And we have a right to know, too."

"You'll have to explain this to your parents when you return," Priya insisted. The downcast eyes were a clue Amelie wasn't pleased at the prospect.

"I guess that explains partly why I couldn't sense you until you made a noise," Susan added. "Interesting. Must have something to do with the blending of the parent genes. It's certainly not a lab-invented attribute as this child has never been in the lab."

"What else can you do?" Priya asked. "Other than become invisible and sneak aboard our copter to follow us here. And what can your brother do?"

"We both know how to change shapes," Amelie beamed. She stood up and prepared for another demonstration. Reaching her arms high above her head, she stretched as much as she could, until her form fizzled from human child to giraffe.

"Wow!" both sisters exclaimed.

"And George?" Priya asked.

"He's cat and lion like our parents. Nothing special."

"How did you get the giraffe gene?"

She shrugged. "I don't know. Perhaps the same as my invisibility gene."

"Amazing."

"So, back to the questions. Why did you sneak aboard the 'copter and follow me here?" Priya asked, all sternness again.

"I wanted to be with you. I wanted to see D'Sonoqua." She glanced at Susan. "It's you, isn't it?" Susan nodded. "Wow! I'm related to the wild woman of the woods."

The three shared a laugh.

Clearing her throat, Priya scolded again, "You know it was wrong to sneak aboard. To follow me. Your parents will be worried when they notice you missing."

Amelie let loose a deep sigh of resignation. "You can speak to Mother in your mind, Aunt Priya, and let her know I'm here with you."

She did just that. *She's here, Kat. Priya's here with me. And Amell's other sister.*

"You told her, didn't you? What did she say?" Amelie asked.

"Nothing. Yet. But I'm sure she'll have plenty to say when we return.

Amelie crossed her arms in front of her and allowed her face to conjure up a pout. It didn't work. Especially when her two aunts started chuckling. She had to join in. Laughter is always good medicine.

Priya broke the spell by clearing her throat. "Amelie. I expect you to do as we say and sit there quietly until we're finished our discussion."

"Yes, Aunt Priya." Another coy smile.

Turning her attention back to Susan, Priya asked, "Why here? Why hide?"

"I have nowhere else to go," Susan's voice was laced with regret. Sorrow. "Where could I go? Looking like this." And she waved her hands in the air, emphasizing her looks from head to toe. "I didn't change right away. I once was human looking. Then I found my ability to change. Only, unlike you, I couldn't change back. Something about the chemicals they poured into my system. This is the form I must endure for the length of my existence."

"That's horrible." Priya was genuinely shocked. "I hadn't realized…" She left her sentence dangling.

"Of course." Susan nodded her head in agreement. "Why should you? After all, you've only been made aware of your abilities recently. And you've only just met some of the others. Not all to be trusted, but there are some good ones in the bunch. You'll learn to detect whom to trust. Hopefully sooner, rather than later."

"But why don't you join Amell and I and the others at Castle Mutasim?" Priya asked. "No one would judge your appearance at the castle."

"Some would," Susan explained. "I did try. But something about my form requires, no demands, a natural habitat. And isolation."

Priya felt sad for her sister. Doomed for life as an outcast. Alone. She wiped away a tear which was trickling down her cheek. For Susan. For herself. For all the other mutants, both at the castle and still undergoing horrendous procedures in the various lab facilities around the world. It didn't make sense. Nothing made sense.

"Don't trouble yourself about me," Susan broke through Priya's thoughts. "Or about the others either. We are what we are and we have to learn to accept it. To live with it."

Priya sniffled. Wiped her cheeks with the cuff of her sleeve, oblivious to her niece's shocked expression at witnessing an older person doing something children are always told not to do. "But you haven't explained why you captured me," Priya pushed her point forward. "Why the staged kidnapping?"

Susan shrugged her shoulders. That, and the grin, must be a couple of her nervous quirks. She certainly did the two often enough. "I wanted to meet my sister. And I wanted you alone. Away from them."

"Wayne? Roderick? You keep suggesting I can't trust them. Why?"

"The lab creators want you all back in their control. They've implanted many with untraceable devices only they can monitor. They know where you are, Priya. You will never be safe until the problem is rooted out for good." Susan shifted her weight, leaning slightly to the side. She reached down and gave her rump a good scratch. Noticing Priya's discomfort, she chuckled. Or, at least, Priya assumed it was a chuckle. It sounded more like a gagging chihuahua. "Sorry. This thick fur is a nest for all manner of annoying critters. I've tried shaving it off, but to no avail. It grows back in less than a day, usually thicker than what I shaved off. I've tried bathing in the freshwater springs nearby. It only matts the fur into miserable knots that provide nests for those incessant critters. It's a useless battle. So, I quit. And, I scratch. I'll never be a social butterfly in human circles, that's for sure." And she chortled another gasping laugh.

Priya shook her head, more in disbelief than shock. How could anyone manipulate life in such an insufferable manner? So blatantly ignore the laws of nature and make life unbearable for some while benefiting only a few others? It was inconceivable. And, yet, it was the core of humanity: greed at all cost. "I'm so sorry, Susan. Really, I am."

"Humph!" Susan let out a deep-throated grunt. "I know you are, Priya. It's not your fault. But perhaps you can assist in finding a resolution. This has been going on for centuries, long before Europeans invaded this land and claimed it as their own. They, those who created us, are not human. But they must be destroyed. Before more of us, before more Sasquatch and D'Sonoqua's and who knows what else, roam the earth and terrorize, or worse, the rest of the world of purebred humans and purebred other animal forms."

"Tell me," Priya pondered aloud. "I want to know. I'm sure Amelie does, too. About D'Sonoqua. The legend. How many there were before you. How many there are now. And how old are you?"

Susan let out a deep-throated bellow. She was laughing, Priya was sure of it. It rocked the body of D'Sonoqua. It rocked the ground on which they sat. It shattered the air around them, sending birds of all sizes scattering amongst the trees. She laughed until tears dripped from the corners of the eyes. Down the furry cheeks, dampening a channel around the cheekbones. Priya and Amelie watched. Transfixed with a mixture of horror and awe.

When the laughter eased, Priya asked, meekly, "What was so funny?"

"You." The creature coughed. Chuckled some more. Coughed again. Then cleared her throat. "You and all your questions." She cleared her throat again. "You do realize women never reveal their age." And she chortled an extended laugh. "Oh my!" She wiped a paw across the eyes. Sniffled. Breathed deeply. Then spoke with unexpected calm. "I'm not the original D'Sonoqua. There have been many. I am the most recent. Currently there are at least a dozen of us. Escapees, if you will. Living in the rough. Avoiding human contact for fear of being discovered, captured and re-incarcerated. As for my age? Not much older than you. As I said, we are related, in a way. You, me and Amell." Priya startled at the mention of her brother. "I helped him hide for a time, you know."

"Wow!" Priya exclaimed. "He did mention receiving help from other escapees."

"Would you have believed him if he told you about me? Told you that you were related to D'Sonoqua?" An eyebrow arched upward. "After all, you've only just discovered who you are. What you are."

"Probably not." Priya sat quietly, pondering. It had been a confusing, complicated few weeks. First venturing far from the only home she'd known. Or, at least, could remember. The accident. Waking up miles from her intended destination to discover her long-lost brother. Learning she was a mutant. Learning her beloved dog, Bear, was a mutant. Learning there were many other mutants. It had been, to say the least, overwhelming. And, not a tad, unbelievable. Far-fetched, to put it bluntly. Had someone told her months ago, when she applied for the advertised position, she'd be training to transform into multiple alternate forms, she would have laughed in the person's face. No, she wouldn't have believed D'Sonoqua existed, let alone was her sister.

Susan nodded in understanding. "I thought not. The First Nations people, the Kwakwaka'wakw and many of the other tribes, frequently witnessed mutants. Some of the Kwakwaka'wakw were even mutants themselves. It's all recorded in their legends and their art. The fabulous totem poles have animals representing the Kwakwaka'wakw other forms. They knew of the transformation process. They just didn't understand they had been created in a lab."

"By aliens," Priya added. "The they," she used her fingers to air quote the last word, "everyone talks about are aliens, aren't they?"

A deep throated sigh was the creature's only response. They sat quietly for some time, deep in their own thoughts. Finally, Susan broke the stalemate of silence which engulfed them. She shuffled over to Priya and wrapped her in her arms. A sisterly hug. Surprised, Priya studied her captor's face, looking for clues to help her understand.

"You'll leave when you're ready," Susan explained simply. "I have spoken to my sister. All is good. Your men are closer, but they'll never find us here. Too high; too steep an incline; too secluded. But you'll want to join them soon." She sat back.

Priya didn't move. "Is there anything any of us can do to reverse what they did to you and the others?"

Susan chortled and coughed, glancing briefly at Priya and then Amelie, before darting her eyes all around, avoiding contact of any sort. "No. I doubt it. But we can stop them from doing more experiments. From creating more lab-induced mutants."

"Why are they doing this?"

"Because they can, I suppose." Another shrug of the shoulders. "Who knows? Perhaps they're working on a super-army to take over the world. Or, to sell to the highest bidder. There's always money involved. Somehow. Money and greed for power. I just want it stopped. Tell Amell, we're all ready when he is. Just give the signal."

Priya gasped. Her brother had planned this all along. This wasn't a break from study and training. This wasn't a pleasure visit to a First Nations' community, to understand the mutants past and present. This was a ploy for her to meet their sister, Susan, or D'Sonoqua. To assess the situation. To see if they were willing and ready. But for what? "The signal? What signal?"

"He'll know."

Rustling from below startled the two. "You'd best go before they find me. They can't be trusted. Or, at least one of them can't." Susan rolled onto all fours and crawled into an opening in the cliff-side, one Priya hadn't noticed earlier because of the rocks and shrubs hiding its position. After the last rear paw disappeared, Susan's head poked out, "Go! Now! I've enjoyed meeting you, Sis. We'll meet again."

There was more rustling from below. Closer. Standing up, she motioned her niece closer. "Feel like flying?" she asked, giving her own version of a coy smile.

"Sure," Amelie beamed.

"Wrap your arms around my neck and hold on tight," Priya instructed as she spread her arms. "I've never done this before. Never carried anyone in flight. But at least you don't weigh too much."

With her niece wrapped around her neck, Priya spread her arms and jumped, hoping the cramped feelings from being tied up would dissipate once she was airborne. Hoping she didn't drop her precious cargo. She swooped over the area, coming back to reassess the position. She wanted to be sure she could find this cave again. To find Susan. Her sister. Then she swooped down and breezed above Wayne's head. Startled, he glanced up, in the process, losing his footing and tumbling back down the slope. Priya started to giggle, but realized Wayne's predicament was dire. She swooped lower and reached out to grab his shoulders, to prevent him from falling to an uncertain demise. Now she would have to carry two people: a child and an adult. She had no choice. The alternative was dire.

CHAPTER TWENTY-THREE

"You can't rush these things, Priya," Wayne spoke with calm reverence. He was always calm. It was part of his canine genes: calm and soothing. Not to mention forever devoted. He rubbed his shoulder where the claws of his rescuer had dug deeply. "Next time you try to save me, Priya," he grumbled, "don't clench so hard."

Priya merely giggled softly in return. "You have to remember I was carrying another precious cargo at the same time. I didn't want to lose either of you." The two were walking around the courtyard near the rampart walls, taking an evening stroll as had become a habit. Others were out and about doing their thing, leaving Wayne and Priya to some alone time. Following their short sojourn to Gwa'yasdams, the training had resumed with renewed fervor. The daytime hours were packed full of training exercises and study. It was nothing like the librarian/archivist job Priya thought she'd applied for.

Amelie received some discipline from her parents and was confined to the children's quarters for a few days. Priya had to admit she missed the little charmer. She wondered what Amell and Kat thought of their daughter's talents, particularly the invisibility one. Priya had sat with the family group, insisting Amelie reveal all. No more secrets. Amelie, coy and manipulative, tried to weasel out of the confession, but Priya hadn't backed down. There was too much at stake. If Amelie entrapped herself in a dangerous setting by using her ability to become invisible, who knew what might happen. The grounding action, a typical tactic of many parents gave both parents and child time to reflect. Amell and Kat were beside themselves with worry, not knowing how to deal with this new revelation. And it opened the question, what other talents was Amelie hiding? And her brother, for that matter.

"I want to shut them down, Wayne!" Her voice was insistent. She had told Wayne and Roderick nothing about her visit with D'Sonoqua, other than finding their stowaway clinging to the cliffside. The entire trip back to Castle Mutasim was a barrage of questions from the men which met with stony silence from Priya and a few muffled giggles from her niece. She had a lot to think about. As soon as they returned, she ushered Amelie into the library where the parents awaited. Once Amelie had been dealt with, Priya retreated to her room, waiting for her brother. She knew he would come for his message. After all, he was the one who had sent her to receive the message. She hadn't been disappointed. Although, his only response was a slight nod of the head. Later, at dinner, he had announced the new regimen for everyone to follow. The training was ramped up significantly for everyone, leaving no doubt the tactical moment was quickly approaching.

"I feel I'm ready," she told Wayne, still reluctant to share anything with him. Not with Roderick, either. She didn't know who she could trust anymore. "I know the others are. They've trained longer and harder than I have."

"Amell has scouts surveying the area around the lab," Wayne noted, taking Priya's hand in his and tugging her, gently, a little closer. "The intel coming back here suggests something big is about to happen. What? We don't know. But we're holding back until we know more."

"We can't hold back forever."

"Patience, Priya. Amell will know when the time is right. And we have to be ready when he gives the call to arms, so to speak."

"Humph!"

Priya was losing patience with this waiting. And the training. And the studying. She wanted action. It felt like months since she arrived at Castle Mutasim. Other than the breach caused by her so-called friends, all had been quiet. Too quiet. Something was up. She could feel it. Sense it. And it unsettled her to the core.

"They're coming, Wayne," she spoke softly. "I know they are. They're very close."

"Perhaps," he replied. "But we're ready for them."

"Are we, Wayne? Are we?"

Wayne dropped Priya's hand and took a step ahead. Turning to face her, he placed his hands on her shoulders and studied her intently, square in the eye. "Priya," he said sternly. "We have to have faith. We have to believe in ourselves and in each other. That's the most important part of our training. If we can't trust ourselves, we won't be ready for anything. You know the saying, *divide and conquer*?" Priya nodded slightly while keeping her eyes locked on Wayne's. "If they can divide us, then they will succeed in conquering us. Again. And we can't risk that. Not for you. Not for me. Not for any of us."

"So, it's *do or die*." Priya threw in another quote.

"When the time comes, Priya. Yes, it is. None of us want to be re-captured and confined to one of their labs and the countless, often painful experiments. At least here, we are free."

"Are we?" She raised an eyebrow to emphasize her query.

"Moreso than we would be in a lab," Wayne answered, a tone of somberness evident in his voice. "You have no idea how bad it is in on of those labs. You've been spared the pain, the confinement, the searing agony of being a pincushion and nothing more."

Priya took a step back, breathing deeply. "I suppose you're right, Wayne. I have never experienced their labs. But I have endured a lot of testing here and some of it was painful. And we are confined for the most part."

Wayne chuckled softly. "Not my little sparrow who's found her wings. You can fly anywhere you want."

"Within reason. If I go too far, the implant Amell insisted installing will give me a shock and tug me back here."

"It's for your protection, Priya," Wayne explained. "If they capture you. Or you're injured. We can track your location and come to your rescue."

She let out another deep breath. "I'm sorry, Wayne. My frustration and impatience is mounting by the day. I just want my old life back. My freedom. My job in the archives. Normalcy."

"It doesn't exist for us, Priya. It never has."

"Humph!" She started to turn to head back inside, then paused. "And I'm not a sparrow, Wayne. To set things straight, my bird gene, as you might describe it, is owl."

"My little night owl, then," Wayne stood corrected. "With the vision we will surely need when we storm the battlements of the lab."

Shaking her head, Priya left Wayne standing beside the battlements and headed inside. She was tired. The grueling training and study was taking its toll on her. She was itching to put it to good use. But she understood the reasoning behind the wait. The planning and the timing were essential. To get things right, one had to plan well and time to perfection.

CHAPTER TWENTY-FOUR

She was stepping into her room when the alarm sounded. Another breach? She didn't stop to ponder. She knew the drill. Her skills for flying with night vision were essential. She galloped toward the stairs and took a flying leap over the railing, landing glibly on the descending rail and sliding the remainder of the way to the ground floor, jumping off with ease before coming to a stop at the newel post. She continued her frantic pace, circling around beyond the library to the hideous stairs leading to the lower control rooms.

The alarm continued to blare, but there were no verbal instructions, as she recalled in earlier exercises. She heard the clicking of locks, but failed to notice any of the monitors projecting images of a breach. And, where was everyone? In her hasty descent, she hadn't encountered a single soul.

Kat. She reached out in her mind. *Kat.* No answer. Emptiness. The castle was empty. A nagging ache tugged at her gut. She slowed her descent, moving with caution. Was it a trap?

A voice pierced above the incessant noise of the alarm. "Self destruct in fifteen seconds."

"What the…?" she muttered. Something was terribly wrong. She knew the final defense was self destruct. It meant the breach was all consuming. Whoever could escape had already done so. Those who remained would incinerate when the castle exploded into the night air.

"Fourteen, Thirteen, Twelve," the countdown was methodical, hauntingly paced. She had a choice. Descend to the control rooms below and risk termination, permanently. Or, soar away through the night sky and find another safe haven. She knew where many of these safe havens were. This castle was only a small part of Amell's network around the world. She could escape. She could find another refuge. But the others? Wasn't there something she could do to help them?

"Sometimes the best thing you can do in the moment is rescue yourself," Amell had stated with firm reverence on multiple occasions.

The children! Her mind exploded in panic. *Where are the children? Are they safe? Is Amelie safe?* She had to know. She couldn't leave without first checking upstairs in the children's space.

"Amelie," she called out as she raced up the stairs, spreading her arms to take flight. She had come to realize there were times when flying could be so much more efficient and effective than running. And this was one of them.

She soared above the stairs, through the halls, up another flight of stairs until she reached the top floor. She placed her feet firmly on the floor and settled back into her human form.

"Eleven. Ten." She was running out of time. The doors were ajar.

"Amelie. George. Children." She called out using her strongest voice. No response. Should she be relieved? She wasn't sure. A sound from behind startled her.

"Aunt Priya." It was Amelie.

Priya turned abruptly, snatched up the child who had materialized behind her and started a hasty descent. The only window she knew she could open easily was in her room. Best take their chances there than risk time trying the other windows. As she ran, she spat out a barrage of questions, including, "What are you doing here? Where are the others?"

"Everyone left. Earlier. Just you, me and Wayne."

"Wayne. Where is he?" She gasped, concern and exertion causing her air consumption to multiply. There was no time to look for him. He would have to make his own escape. If he could.

"How did the others know to escape? Where did they go? And why are you still here?" They had reached her bedroom. Priya pushed the door open and made for the window.

Calm as could be, Amelie answered the questions in order. "Mother said they received a warning tip. To escape while they could. To a safe place far from here. I'm not sure exactly where it is. I stayed behind to warn you. To protect you. I didn't want you left behind. They were leaving you behind, Aunt Priya. With Wayne. He's bad. They said he was bad."

"No. He can't be. He protected me." Priya wrapped her arms around the girl. "Hold on tight. Like you did when we left Susan on the mountain cliff." The girl wrapped her arms tight around Priya's neck, latching on so the owl could take flight.

She had plenty of questions. Answers she'd demand from her brother when they met again. And they would meet again. She was sure of it. Particularly the question of how this had come to such a final conclusion so quickly? Right now, she had to find Wayne. She had to make sure he was safe. The last she'd seen him, was only moments ago, in the courtyard below. She'd swoop across the area and take a quick look before the countdown was complete.

"Six. Five. Four." No time left.

With a flying leap, she dashed through the window and spread her wings soaring through the open window. Outside. Free. She pumped her wings to gain height. Upwards she went before banking around to the right and doing an about turn to swoop down into the ramparts. She saw him.

"Wayne!" she called, her voice coming out like an owl's call, somewhere between a bark and a trill. She felt her niece bury her head in the feathers around the neck. She was almost a full owl now. In full combat mode. Protecting her loved ones.

"Wayne," she called out as she glided downward.

He saw her. Shaking his head, he waved frantically, calling out, "Save yourself."

She opened her claws as her human hands morphed into her owl appendages and made a dive. Amelie clung even tighter. As she approached the man-dog mutant, she stretched her limbs and clasped the claws over his shoulders. Wayne let out a yelp as he transformed into his other genetic makeup: dog. She had him in her grip and he was feeling the pinch of her claws. She channelled her strength to gain altitude, as fast as possible, to carry them above the rampart walls and into the woods beyond.

Wayne squirmed and howled, but Priya managed to maintain her grip as she cleared the rampart walls with ease. Climbing ever higher, she soared over the tree tops, and into the night sky, making haste to put as much distance between them and the doomed castle as possible. The voice of the countdown echoed in her ears as it reached the final numbers. And then, an explosion like no other ripped through the night sky, rumbling the earth beneath her and lighting up like a massive dome. She was sure the noise and the light show would be heard and seen miles away.

Other than a quick glance back, she kept her pace, still wanting to increase the distance between her and what remained of Castle Mutasim. She felt her eyes water up, but she didn't give in. This was no time for tears. Over the weeks of living at the castle, she'd become fond of it and its inhabitants. Now, in a blink of an eye, it was gone. And where were all the inhabitants? Where was Amell? Kat? The others? Were they safe? Or captured? And was this all because they wanted to get her. She cringed thinking of the danger she had carried into the once safe and secure castle. It was her doing. All hers. It was time to set things right. Time to get rid of them!

She could feel the cramps before she felt the fatigue. She wasn't used to flying so long, so high, so fast, and carrying a double load at the same time. At least Wayne had settled down, allowing her to transport the three of them to safety. She had to set down. Slowing her pace, she circled a clear-cut disaster left behind by a logging company. She soared in, making way for what remained of the treeline. Once she was a foot above the ground, she let go of her clasp and Wayne tumbled, rolling in the dirt. She set down a few feet away, folding her wings to her side.

CHAPTER TWENTY-FIVE

Priya and Wayne transformed into their human forms and sat where they had dropped, panting and catching their breaths. Amelie rolled away, but not before her own scolding reached Priya's ears. "You should have left him behind. He's bad." The voice was soft, meant only for her aunt's ears. Priya glanced at Wayne nervously, wondering if he'd heard. If he had, he made no mention of it.

When Wayne spoke, it shattered the silence, causing Priya to jump. "Wow! That was amazing! Again. And with little Amelie. Again. What a ride."

Priya chuckled softly, rubbing her arms vigorously. "Easy for you to say. You should try carrying a seventy plus pound dog above the treetops for miles and miles on end. With a little girl wrapped around my neck, clinging for life. My arms are throbbing. My entire body is screaming in pain." She whimpered as her rubbing hit an exceptionally tender spot.

"Come here," Wayne shuffled toward her. "If there's one thing I'm good at, it's massaging sore muscles. Lord knows I've had more than my share of aches and pains, changing to a dog that loves to run and jump, then back to the human form. One thing they never considered was the strain these changes make on the body."

Priya pivoted toward Wayne, holding out the right arm, the one which ached the most. As Wayne rubbed and prodded, she closed her eyes, allowing her body to relax, to soak up the attention and the loosening of the strained muscles. As the pain eased, she let out a deep sigh. "Any idea where we are?" she asked in a half whisper.

"Somewhere on Vancouver Island," Wayne gave a short response, not pausing in his massage strokes.

"It narrows it down." She moaned in relief as he set down the right arm and reached for the left one to repeat the process. "You're good at this."

"Told you."

"So, where's the closest safe place?"

"You're assuming there is one."

"There has to be. Amell and the others wouldn't settle for just one safe place. Just one Castle Mutasim. There has to be others."

"I do know of one other," Wayne admitted. "Amell didn't share every safe place to every inhabitant of the castle. There were spies amongst us. Even the mutants were compromised and controlled by them."

"Where is this safe place?"

"Northern Alberta."

"Near the lab?"

"It is the lab."

"You're one of them," Priya slid back in disgust. "You're one of the spies."

"Told you," Amelie muttered from where she still sat, observing the intimacy with disgust.

"You shut up," Wayne snapped at the girl.

"Wayne!" Priya exploded. "Don't talk like that. And to Amelie. So rude."

He snorted in response. Returning his attention to Priya's arm, he dug his fingers into the flesh with unnecessary force.

"Ouch!" Priya shrieked, pulling her arm away from him. "Enough. I can't believe you're a traitor. Susan warned me."

"Who's Susan?" He shook his head as if he didn't care. "Never mind this Susan. I am what I am. I didn't want to be, Priya." Wayne whined like a sick puppy. "You have to believe me. They controlled me. Totally."

"And Amell didn't know?"

"He knew. And he used me to his benefit."

"So, they're all safe. Somewhere. But not at the lab."

"Perhaps not all safe. I don't know how many escaped this time. Amell wanted me destroyed in the self-destruct. I wanted to be destroyed, too. But you decided to rescue me."

"Did he want me destroyed as well?" Priya shuddered as the thought invaded her mind. "I'm his sister. I thought he cared for me. Yet he left me behind. With you. Alone in a castle set to self destruct."

"He knew you'd fly away to your freedom," Wayne assured her. "He used you to keep me distracted while the others escaped. He never thought you'd try, let alone be successful, in rescuing me."

"But I did. And now what?"

"I must do what I've been instructed to do, Priya," he proclaimed. "I'm to take you to the lab. It should have happened after the accident in Yukon. But it didn't. Amell reached you first. It should have happened when your friends arrived at Castle Mutasim. But they were captured and you know the rest. You've been wanting to go there. Haven't you, Priya? Now, I must take you there."

Priya glanced around nervously. Lights flickered in the forest growth around them. "It's them, isn't it, Wayne? They've come for us. For me. For Amelie. Haven't they? You've betrayed me. You, who were supposed to protect me. You, who possesses the genes of the most loyal and devoted creature walking this earth. How could you? How could you put me in danger? And threaten poor Amelie as well?"

"They made me, Priya," he confessed, reaching out toward her. She slid back, further away from him, shaking her head in disgust. "Yes, it's them. They've come to take us both home. Amelie, too. A bonus they weren't expecting. Home to the lab."

"No!" Priya shoved herself off the ground, taking a step back. Wayne's grip on her arm tightened. "No!" she screamed. "Let me go!"

Some invisible force slammed into Wayne. He lost his grip. Turned around swinging at whatever had attacked him. There was nothing. No one.

Priya seized the moment and spread her arms, preparing for flight. She made a dash up the slope. Away from Wayne. Away from the approaching them. "Amelie," she called out. "Amelie." She sensed movement but saw nothing. Then a force wrapped its body around hers.

"I'm here, Aunt Priya. Let's go. He's coming."

A reassuring voice gave Priya the momentum she needed to lift off. She didn't need to look to know who was close. Too close. She ran faster, arms spread and left the ground behind, Amelie wrapped securely against her body. A force tugged at her legs, dragging her down. Wayne. It had to be him. No one else was close enough to target her legs. She shook frantically but was unable to disengage.

"Let go, Wayne," she yelled as she flew even higher.

"Not going to happen, Priya. Time to go home."

She flew around the perimeter of the clear-cut fields, noting the droves of approaching lights. The enemy. Them. Circling, she dove into the center of the field, as low as she dared, hoping to drag Wayne's body enough that he would have to release his grip. The stumps of logs provided the perfect props and she dragged him relentlessly toward one after another, ignoring his shrieks of agony. Finally, he let go.

Free, Priya flew up higher before Wayne could latch on again. Only then did she notice her weight load had lessened. "Amelie!" she screamed. Circling the field again, the enemy tightening its noose more significantly, she noticed Wayne grasping hold of the girl. "Amelie!" she screamed again. She would not allow her niece, her brother's child, to be their newest lab rat.

"I have her, Priya," Wayne yelled upward, his voice underlined with a growl as his dog gene fought for control. "Come down here and she'll not be harmed."

Oh yes! The words swirled inside her head. *I'll come down there all right. And you'll be sorry you messed with me.* Her anger knew no bounds. It took the panicked voice of a child to stop her escape. "Aunt Priya. Help!"

The last remaining untested owl gene kicked in, the predator instinct. She plunged to the earth, aiming at Wayne in attack mode. Without Priya's night vision, he couldn't see clearly the manner of her approach. Her feet were now claws, stretched talons, long and sharp, her face sported a strong, spiked beak. Wayne was her prey and he would rue the day he took advantage of her, threatening her and those she loved.

Her talons dug into Wayne's torso moments before the beak jabbed the face. Around the eyes, the cheeks, the ears. Priya was vicious. Relentless. Wayne growled as his body became a dog. He nipped back at the owl attacker. But Priya was more agile than she thought possible. She released her grip and flew upward. High. Out of reach.

Wayne still had Amelie in his grasp. His face marred the once placid best friend he had been. Now he was the predator and Amelie his victim. He wouldn't eat her, would he? Priya wasn't about to wait to find out.

She did a full circle of the field, taking in the approaching storm of 'them'. She would have to be quick. Brutal. She let out an ear-piercing screech and dove into her target, talons poised, beak well aimed. Wayne might have been expecting another attack, but he obviously didn't expect the ferocity of this one. With her talons, Priya clutched and grabbed and jerked the fully formed dog with brutal force. With her beak, she pierced Wayne's face and eyes with relentless jabs. He shrieked in response, curling his body away, trying to make his own escape. In the process, he released the girl.

Without pause in the attack, Priya instructed her niece, "Latch on, Amelie. Quickly." Once she felt the child's weight around her neck, she ceased the attack and soared upward. Away from the approaching enemy. Away from the one she had trusted and started to love. It was a painful parting of ways.

Priya and her passenger soared through the night sky. Away from Wayne. Away from the heartache he caused. Away from the danger he presented. Away from everyone and everything. She flew ever higher, ever further away from the tiny barking, growling figure frantically yapping at her as she soared along the coast and vanished into the thick rainforests which hadn't yet been destroyed by loggers. It was as she surged into the treetops that she heard the unmistakeable roar of a helicopter, hovering closer by the minute. They were tracking her. She sensed lasers directed at her, but she felt nothing. She flew harder, weaving deeper into the thickness of the forest, searching for something, someplace safe, somewhere to hide until they gave up and moved on.

CHAPTER TWENTY-SIX

She didn't know how long she flew, but she was tiring quickly. Amelie was becoming a dead weight, pulling her down. She wondered if the girl had dozed off. She would have to find a safe landing place. Soon. If Amelie was asleep, she might loosen her grip and fall. Besides, Priya wasn't sure she had the strength to carry on much further.

The pursuant sounds had long since dissipated. Could she hope they were gone? That they had lost her scent? Her trail? Would she ever be safe in this world? Why was she so important to them? Whoever they or them was.

So many questions. *And you shall have the answers.* It was Kat. She was speaking inside her head. Finally.

Where are you?

Close.

I have Amelie.

I thought you might. That's a relief.

How much further?

Not far. Waiting for you. Waiting until they lost your trail. You're near. Sissy will come and escort you to us. Look off to your left. There she is.

The communication ceased. There was no further need. Priya saw Sissy as the hawk soared closer. Vying off in the opposite direction than Priya had headed, the two wove through and above the thick forests until Sissy swooped down toward what appeared to be a secluded beach. In spite of her night vision, which was fading with her growing fatigue, it was difficult to tell in the dark with no moonlight. The night sky was overcast, dark, dreary and threatening. Good camouflage, but not so good for making a safe get-away.

Sissy landed on the beach, transforming to her human form as Priya followed close behind. Amelie stirred and released her grip on Priya, stifling a yawn.

"Where are we?" she asked, still groggy.

"Close to a safe place," Sissy responded.

"Sissy?" the girl yawned again. "Do we have to walk? I'm so tired."

"Can you carry her, Sissy?" Priya asked, stifling some yawns herself. "I'm plumb worn out."

"No problem. Let's go." The women, both human again, stood up and brushed the sand and grit from their bodies. Sissy reached down and gathered Amelie in her arms, the girl already fast asleep. Again.

"This way," Sissy whispered, as she marched away from the water's edge toward the treeline. They didn't talk. There was no need. As long as Priya could see the dark shadow of her guide, all she needed was to know there was a safe place nearby.

Poking through the thick undergrowth, the two climbed a steep incline, reaching an opening in the rockface just as Priya was beginning to collapse with fatigue.

"In here," Sissy spoke softly over her shoulder.

Priya wasn't sure about the dark, cavernous opening. Was she finally safe? Or was this another trap? At this point, she was too tired to care. And she wanted some answers. Now. Kat promised. And Priya was determined to hold her friend accountable for those promised answers.

It's safe, Priya. Come in with Sissy. Kat spoke through Priya's unshared concerns. Following Sissy through the opening, she allowed her owl eyes to take control, seeing what others would not be able to see in this intense, black darkness. She was able to follow Sissy's shadow as she made her way through a tight space toward another opening in the rocky crevice. Sissy squeezed through, not an easy manoeuvre with a child in her arms, and disappeared on the other side. Priya followed, keeping her eyes peeled for anything suspicious. Not that it would help as everything appeared suspicious, unfamiliar as it was.

She found herself alone in a slightly larger space. She stood still, allowing her eyes to seek another opening, something which would lead her forward, hopefully to someplace safe. Secure. Voices, distant and garbled were filtering through a shadowy space in the corner. Another crevice to crawl through? Priya made her way toward the sound.

"Sissy. Kat. Amell." She called out, softly at first, then repeated it again slightly louder.

You're almost there, Priya. Another crevice to crawl through.

Feeling along the smooth rock wall, she found the break wrapped around another space, leading her to a hidden crevice. There was a ribbon of light emitting through the space beyond. She followed the light, barely able to squeeze through this opening. She had no idea how Sissy managed with her bundle. As Priya emerged on the other side, the rock face behind her rolled into place, sealing off the opening. Protection? Or imprisonment?

She didn't have time to ponder. As she walked closer to the light, a figure jumped out of the shadows. It was Kat. In her feline form. She quickly morphed into her human shape and wrapped Priya in a hug. Turning to Sissy, she gathered Amelie into her arms.

"Thank God you're safe!" she proclaimed, stepping back. Studying her mate's sister intently, she added, "Amell was beside himself with worry. He didn't want to leave you behind. He wasn't sure if you were ready to take charge. To do the right thing. To escape before the castle imploded. And then we discovered Amelie missing. We knew she had slipped into invisibility mode, staying behind to be with you. We could only hope she found you and the two of you were able to escape."

"More like exploded," Priya corrected. "I did manage. Carried Amelie and Wayne miles from the site only to discover he was a traitor."

"Yes. We couldn't tell you about him," Kat's voice displayed regret. "I argued that we should tell you, but Amell was swayed by the others. Especially as you and Wayne were becoming so close. We didn't know for sure how compromised you were."

"How long have you known about Wayne?"

"Long enough. But come. Amell will explain the rest. You must be exhausted. And famished."

As if to emphasize the point, Priya's stomach let out a roar of protest. It would have to be food first, answers second.

Kat chuckled softly. "Sissy will lead you. I'll take care of our little bundle here and join you shortly." She left the two alone, sneaking off down another darkened tunnel.

Sissy led Priya through a twisted arrangement of tunnels and open spaces, each turn bringing them into another space more brightly lit than the previous. The path began to descend and, with one last turn, the two paused at an open space which rivalled the grand dining room of Castle Mutasim. And, yes, it sported a long table, not so different from the castle's dining table, which, of course, was laden with platters of food. Everyone, it appeared, was present, grabbing food, glancing around and chatting up a storm. Everyone except Wayne.

Amell stepped forward and, before Priya realized his presence, pulled his sister into a big hug. "Thank God you're safe," he proclaimed. "I would never have forgiven myself had something happened to you." Priya felt his body shudder beneath the embrace. "And Amelie?"

"Safe," Priya responded. "Kat took her to the children's rooms, I assume, to settle her for the night."

"That's a relief." He hugged his sister even tighter, until she squealed at the restriction of airflow to her lungs.

It was Roderick clearing his throat which startled the two to step back. "Welcome to our new home," he announced. "It's not Castle Mutasim. Yet. We can always build another castle, but, for now, this is home. Safe and secure underground."

Kat slipped into the room, sidling up to Amell and Priya. "Amelie didn't blink an eye, all settled into her new bed."

"That was quick." Priya couldn't hide the tone of surprise in her voice.

"It wasn't far," Kat explained. "We're keeping the children closer to us. For their protection as much as our peace of mind. They would love to get their hands on our children. And we can't let that happen." She reached out to Priya and pulled her into an embrace. "Thank you for caring for our daughter and bringing her safely back to us. To our new underground castle." Priya felt Kat shudder under their embrace. Knowing how much her brother's mate despised the deep underground, she patted her shoulders offering reassurance and sisterly compassion. Kat stood back, sniffling. "Thanks," she mouthed for Priya's eyes only.

Roderick cleared his throat again. "Can we eat now?" His words brought a resounding roar of laughter from around the room. "We can always talk while we eat."

"Forever thinking of your stomach, aren't you, Roderick?" Amell bellowed, walking over to pound the hunger magnet on the back.

"Of course," was the expected response. "What else is there to think of?" More laughter shook the cavern.

Everyone moved in, filling their platters high with food. Even Priya grabbed more than she thought she needed, but managed to wolf it all down. As stomachs filled, eating slowed and Priya took the initiative to break the silence.

CHAPTER TWENTY-SEVEN

"How long have you known about Wayne?" she asked, directing the question at no one in particular. "And why didn't someone tell me?"

"You were getting too close to him," Kat took the initiative to answer. "He could sense things. It was his canine gene. He would know if you knew. You wouldn't be able to pretend around him. We had to keep him under surveillance, and we had to make sure he didn't suspect that we knew."

"So, you used me." Priya shook her head, placing her cutlery on the empty plate and pushing it away from her. "You could have exposed him and eliminated the threat. Instead you played with my feelings. You hurt me. He hurt me." She was overwhelmed with emotion. Standing up with haste, she knocked her chair over. She wanted to run. But where? And she was so tired. Everyone was using her and she was tired of being used.

I understand. Kat confessed inside Priya's head. *More than you can imagine. I understand.* Her voice soothed Priya's raging emotions. She knew it was mostly fatigue taking control of her feelings. She wasn't one to vent, usually keeping her thoughts closed inside her. But she was reaching a boiling point. So many questions. So few answers.

"I need answers to my questions," she glared at each one sitting around the table. One at a time. Allowing her eyes to rest briefly on the now familiar faces before moving to the next one. And, finally, her eyes came to rest on her brother, whose face appeared contorted with guilt. As he should be. "Now!" she emphasized. "Starting with Wayne. Why was he inserted in my home, my life and my heart? And now you tell me he was a spy?"

Roderick cleared his throat. He glanced at Amell for assurance before jumping into the fray. "He wasn't compromised initially. At least, we don't think he was." he claimed. Holding up his hand to stop further questions, he rushed into his explanation, not allowing for Priya to interrupt. "We grew up together. In the lab. We escaped together. Amell rescued us off the street. Brought us to one refuge then another after the first refuge was breached. We think, all of us here, that Wayne was altered when they invaded your home in Victoria. You will recall the time you came home to a mess and then you were served a complaint from bylaw about a barking dog?" Priya nodded. "That's when they invaded your space, knocked Wayne out and inserted something new and almost undetectable in his system. As well as other decoys to make us believe the implants had been removed. But this one. It was deep. Right in the center of the brain. There was no way our systems could detect it, let alone remove it. After the breach when your friends invaded and then Samantha self-destructed, we were able to upgrade our tracking technology and we had everyone tested. You will recall you were tested at the time and had some implants removed?" Priya nodded again. "When we tested Wayne, we located the remaining implant. Amell chose not to tell him, hoping we could use this device to further test them and their technology. Unfortunately, we couldn't tell you as we worried it would alert Wayne and, consequently, them. We wanted them to believe they were secure with their monitoring device."

"It was a mean thing to do," Priya sniffled. "How could you? It hurts, you know. It hurts to discover you deceived me and you let Wayne lead me along in a sentimental way." Plopping back into the chair she had vacated, she sniffled again, overwhelmed with a sense of defeat.

Kat reached an arm around Priya and hugged her close. "We know. I argued on your behalf, but there was no other way. We couldn't remove the implant as it was so precariously implanted in the brain. And we couldn't deactivate it. At least, not yet. Perhaps some day."

"How much of Wayne's affections can I trust as genuine? Or were they using my attraction to lure me in? To capture me? To entrap me? To lock me up in a laboratory? In a cage?" She was ranting and she knew it. But she couldn't stop. Her anger was mounting with each question posed, froth and spittle ejecting from her mouth as her words spat out the vehemence she felt. "Tell me!" she yelled her final cadenza, banging her fists on the table. "Tell me! I need to know! I have the right to know!" Her head dropped into her hands, still fisted on the table and her sobs racked through the stunned silence which followed her rampage. The table shook and shuddered as the young woman sobbed on.

Kat tried to console her, patting and rubbing her back with a compassionate touch. She even purred in Priya's ear. The sobbing continued, subsiding slightly with each repeated purr. And then she stopped. Her head remained cradled in the fisted hands, but her tears had dried up. After a few minutes, she gave a final sniffle and straightened up. As her head raised, she glanced at the silent compatriots sitting around the table, some with head bowed in reverence, others whose eyes darted nervously around the room, not knowing what to do, what to think, or where to look. Her tear-stained eyes surveyed the stunned response before falling on Roderick's downturned face and, finally, coming to rest on the guilt-ridden face of her brother.

"I'm sorry, Priya," was all he could think to say, before continuing with a lengthy diatribe which almost sounded like a lecture to a malcontent child. "We are not alone in this battle. We are all forced to surrender something of ourselves for the betterment and safety of the whole. It's not your battle being fought, but rather all of ours. And we must fight it together."

"All for one and one for all, like the Musketeers?" Priya couldn't keep the sarcasm from her voice. She understood. She did. Even though it hurt like a scorched knife, she did understand.

"I suppose, Priya," Amell agreed. "We're all sorry to realize your pain. And, believe me when I say it, we share your pain. Not as intense as you feel it, but we share it nonetheless."

She nodded, sniffling and rubbing her nose and eyes with the ends of her sleeve. Kat handed her a tissue and she made good use of it. "Very well. We now know Wayne is a traitor. We know the castle is mere dust in the wind. We know each of us is disposable. I know I am. After all, you did leave me behind to defend myself." She sensed, rather than saw, her brother shudder at those words, but Priya chose to carry on as if she didn't notice. "What else do we know? And where do we go from here?" She surveyed the room again and noticed some eyes perking up. Her storm had passed. For now. Peace was tentative, but attainable. The battle must go on.

CHAPTER TWENTY-EIGHT

The next hour was spent in heated arguments. Roderick was adamant in his belief Wayne was salvageable. Those were his words.

"He's salvageable," Roderick insisted again. "We just have to remove the implant."

"And most of the brain," Sissy pointed out. "He'll be no more than a vegetable when you're done. And who's to say it's the only implant? There may be something else deeper in the brain. Something even more high tech than this device."

"Which type of vegetable would you prefer were you in his shoes?" Roderick was pacing the room, his eyes narrowing as if to shoot daggers at anyone who dared intervene. It was the fox inside him, the wily, cunning, suspicious nature of a prowling fox. "One used by them?" And he waved his hands dramatically in the air around him, his pacing becoming more agitated. "Or a vegetable allowed to live free?"

"Or a dead one?" someone muttered under his breath.

Roderick heard him. His ears were attuned to the slightest sound. "Dead?" He came to an abrupt standstill, glaring down the table at the person who dared mention the third alternative. "Would that be your preference?"

"Come on, Roderick," Kat intervened, weaving her soothing canine magic into the underlying purr of her tone of voice. "No one wants to be dead. Or controlled like some sort of freak. Or brain dead either, for that matter. We're out of choices. For the time being, we have to leave Wayne where and as he is, until such time as we can safely rescue him without compromising the safety of the rest of us. And until such time as we have the means and ability to safely remove the device without doing him irreparable damage."

"Kat's right." Amell stood up, leaning on the table. His pose was one of authority, taking command of the situation. "Until we can do otherwise, or know of a better solution, we must consider Wayne one of them and a danger to all of us. Now, the immediate concern is what do we or can we do next?"

The argument didn't answer Priya's questions. In fact, it only added further questions. She was more confused now than she had been since her first waking hours at Castle Mutasim. She intervened with another question. "Is this the only safe place now the castle is gone?"

Amell turned to his sister. "We have other places around the globe. But Wayne knows about each of those places. This is the only place he doesn't know about. Unless there's others created by those who reside in our various safe homes. And there may well be. Each home, each safe place, has someone in charge who makes decisions on a need-to-know basis. If they have created alternative safe venues, then they have kept it secret from even us, in case we become compromised. Which we have been. But hopefully Wayne is the last of our spies. At least for the moment." He stole a glance around the table, looking for a suspicious facial expression, for darting eyes which might signify guilt. Satisfied all was clear, he continued, "I think the time has come to become the offenders, not the defenders."

"Here. Here." Several voices raised in instantaneous agreement, with fists pounding the table to emphasize the point.

"It's time to take down the labs and rescue more mutants."

"And if we can rescue Wayne?" Priya asked in a shaky voice, not sure she wanted to hear the answer. "If we can remove the implant without making him a vegetable?"

There was stunned silence. Roderick had shared his peace. Others had objected. Amell took the initiative. "We'll do what we can, little sister," he confessed, using the playful childhood name he saved for special situations like this one; situations which needed more consoling than directives. "We'll do what we can."

Priya gave a nod in Amell's direction, allowing her eyes to remain downcast. Kat continued to hold and sooth her, but she was numb to the attention. She only half listened as plans were made.

"We must act on our own," Amell insisted. "The fewer who know our plans, the safer we'll be. We don't know who's compromised in the other safe homes and we don't know what systems they have implemented to listen to shared discussions."

"And we need to act fast," Roderick added with forced determination. "Before they realize most of us survived the self-destruct of Castle Mutasim."

"Wouldn't Wayne know?" Priya perked up. "He was there till the end. He must know he and I were the only ones left behind. And Amelie, of course. And you're sure he doesn't know about this place and the other places?"

"This place was a well guarded secret," Amell responded.

"I thought Castle Mutasim was a well guarded secret," she argued.

"We created Castle Mutasim to look like we believed it was safe and secure, knowing full well its days of being safe were numbered." Amell glanced around the table. "As this place will be as well if we don't act quickly, like Roderick suggests. We have a plan in place. All of us only know what we need to know to enact our specific duties. It is intentional to ensure the overall success of the mission."

"And what about me?" Priya asked. "What is it you want me to do?"

"Get captured," Roderick muttered.

"What?" This was too much. Her brother and her mutant colleagues wanted her captured? Sacrificed? For what purpose?

Roderick cleared his throat before responding. "You were supposed to be captured this time, but you were too ingenious and managed to escape. Now you must be captured for real and taken inside the lab facilities."

"Now we move onto Plan B," Amell took over. "You were implanted when we removed the last of their implants, in the hopes you could lead us inside, past security, overlooking all the codes. Once inside, you will act scared, but, at the same time, you'll be taking note of everything around you, most particularly any code passwords, devices, anything that might assist our entry. No need to talk. Just look. We'll be following your every move."

"Like when the police wire a witness with a hidden recording device," she surmised.

"Exactly."

"Anything else?"

"Don't allow them to lock you up in a cage," Roderick added. "And resist any surgical tests. Don't drink anything and avoid needles."

Priya shrugged her shoulders. "Piece of cake, obviously. Any suggestions how I'm supposed to do that? And not raise suspicion?" She received no answers; she wasn't expecting any.

Amell wrapped up the meeting. "Time to recharge our batteries," he advised. Nodding at Priya, he spoke to Kat. "Will you show Priya to her quarters, Kat?" She nodded in response. "Six hours rest, then we make haste."

Priya followed her brother's mate down numerous halls. *Be ready at a moment's notice,* Kat spoke inside her head. *We'll be going before six hour's time. Well before. Amell merely wants to confuse the enemy, if need be.*

There's still a spy in our midst? Priya asked. Kat didn't answer. She didn't have to.

CHAPTER TWENTY-NINE

Her quarters, such as they were, had been set up the same as at the castle. The only thing missing was the grand windows through which she could swing out on her nocturnal flights. And, of course, the fireplace. It appeared everything was in order. All her belongings were in place. Her home had been moved en masse. But how? When? And how could she not have noticed?

She was about to ask Kat, but she had left. She could ask through her thoughts, but figured it didn't matter how things had been transported to this underground space. Everything was here. Even her journal, left on the bedside table where she had placed it a few nights earlier, after making an entry. She hadn't written in it since.

Sitting on the edge of her bed, she opened to the last page, allowing the pen to slide out of its holding spot. She curled up her legs in front of her and read quietly to herself: *I think I'm in love. Is it possible? This man-dog mutant whom I once thought was a mutt off the streets is so attuned to me, my thoughts and aspirations and inner most feelings.*

Priya wiped away a tear. "No point reading any more," she scolded herself, muttering under her breath. "We all know how this ended."

Picking up the pen which had slid onto the bedcoverings, she entered the date and started writing. *I don't know why I bother. Amell wants me to believe in him and the others and think of the whole group as a positive. I thought I did. Then Wayne turned on me. Now, I really don't know whom to trust and if I really care. I wonder if I should just branch out on my own and totally isolate myself somewhere secluded – like the North Pole. Or could they find me even there? Is anywhere safe? Are anyone's rights honored? What is the purpose of all this? Why do they want to experiment on us? To what purpose? I have to know. I want to know. But at what expense will this knowledge come? I'm to be on alert. Amell says we launch our offensive this very night. Sometime before dawn. Sometime before another spy betrays our plans. How many spies are there? And to what purpose? Why? The meaning of life has challenged philosophers for centuries. I wonder what these philosophers would conclude given our current mutant situation. I wonder if anyone else really knows. Or, are/were these philosophers all part of them that keep us the lab rats confined, imprisoned, tortured?*

She didn't get the opportunity to finish her thoughts. A gentle knock on the door had Priya hastily tucking the pen inside the journal and placing it on her bedside table. Standing up, she started toward the door, then stopped. She picked up the journal and tucked it under the mattress. Not the most secure location. Definitely the most obvious hiding place. But she was starting to question everything about Amell and his crew, about her overall safety and security. And, she wondered, who had read her journal? She wasn't in the habit of leaving it on her bedside table. Too convenient. Someone wanted her to write in it tonight. Someone who, unlike Kat, couldn't read her thoughts. Was the journal rigged, too? Perhaps the best thing to do with it would be to burn it.

Another knock, slightly louder but still inconspicuous, had her pulling the blankets neatly into place, hopefully securing the hiding place. Although, come to think of it, there were probably hidden cameras all around the room, recording her every movement. How quickly she had become so paranoid even her breathing habits were under scrutiny.

She flicked off the lights. It would dim the image of any recording device. Her owl eyesight would give her the night vision she needed. She walked to the door and whispered into the frame, "Who is it?"

"Amell," came the whispered response. "Time to go."

She cracked the door open to see her brother standing on the threshold, fisted hand raised ready to knock if she didn't answer. It was dark, but neither of them needed illumination to see, their mutant genes providing the ability to see well under any lighting condition. She glanced up and down the hall or tunnel or whatever one called the underground passageway. There was no one in sight. "Where is everyone?"

"All in position," Amell explained. "No time for questions. Everyone knows their place and their task. The less they know, the less they can share if under duress. As for us? The less spoken, the less recorded."

So, Amell suspected recording devices as well. Priya stepped into the hall and pulled the door closed behind her. The two made their way along the corridor, in the opposite direction from the path Kat led her earlier. "Where's Kat?" she whispered. Amell didn't answer. *Oh no!* Priya thought, concentrating hard to close down her mind, to prevent Kat or anyone else from sneaking in to eavesdrop on her thoughts. *Is Kat the other spy? Poor Amell. The poor children.* She thought she heard a cat-like chuckle, if cats could chuckle. Perhaps her mind control attempts were having marginal effect in shutting down her mind connection to Kat.

Amell didn't pause. Instead, he picked up the pace. They exited the protection of the caves, walking out onto a cliff. The moon had slipped behind some clouds, moving on its descent toward dawn. It was dark. Rain threatened.

The two paused on the precipice, glancing at the darkness stretched out before them. "Carry me." It was more a demand than a question. Rather presumptuous of Amell, speaking as he was in a voice little more than a whisper.

Believing time was of the essence, Priya merely responded with a bland, "Okay." She didn't wait for further comments. The more they spoke, the more they thought, the more likely Kat or someone else could detect their location and their intentions. She spread her arms high and jumped into the air, the intense fatigue of earlier in the evening having long since dissipated. She soared around the treetops before swerving back toward the cave entrance, toward her brother. Legs stretched, talons clenched in the grab position, she dove in with ease and grabbed her brother by the shoulders. He, in turn, reached up to take hold of her legs, for added leverage, realizing his size and weight might be an added burden.

"Where to?" Priya called down to him, knowing the night air whooshing beneath them would carry her voice far and wide.

"East," came the simple response and she flew toward the rays of morning light beginning to stretch across the eastern horizon. Dawn would come soon.

Priya soared higher, maintaining a firm hold on her brother's shoulders. She swooped above the treetops, flying toward the ever-brightening sky, away from the threatening clouds and emitted intermittent dribbles of cold, wet rain. As she flew across the beaches lining the northeast coast of Vancouver Island, she gazed in awe at the expanse of blue beneath her, dotted with specks of ships, ferries and fishing boats, and the scattering of islands which marked the path across the Strait of Georgia from Comox to Powell River on the mainland. She banked to the right slightly as she followed the mainland river path through the coastal mountains and into the province's interior, banking one way then the other as she coursed through the river valleys.

She reached the end of the mountain range and flew above the rolling, dry plains of the arid, desert-like interior, then onwards through more valleys coursing their path through the Rocky Mountain range. And, then she soared across the rolling plains yet again, this time in northern Alberta, where miles of foothills were dotted with cattle and wildlife, each munching its own path on the journey of life.

"North," Amell called from below. Priya had been taking in the changing landscape, lost in thoughts and concentration, almost forgetting the load she carried in her claws. Startled back to the present, the morning dawn stretching across the foothills, she changed her course and headed north.

CHAPTER THIRTY

It wasn't at all what Priya expected. Amell had her fly north for what seemed like hours, long past the twinkling early morning lights of Edmonton which faded into the sunrise. Long past the military base at Cold Lake. The air was thicker. Colder. Inhospitable. Not at all like the clingy dampness of the rainforests on Vancouver Island.

The landscape stretching below her was covered in short, cropped trees, barely clinging to the dry land holding tenuously to the roots. It wasn't flat like the prairies. Nor was it mountainous like the Rockies. It wasn't even the rolling hills south of Edmonton. It was a mixture of everything. And nothing.

"Down," Amell's voice carried up to her with a panicked suddenness. "Into the trees."

Priya didn't argue, merely following directions. Once she'd positioned her brother on the ground, she settled down herself. That's when the pain of aching muscles set in. She noticed Amell feeling similar discomforts as he rolled and rubbed his shoulders where Priya had clenched with talons. She shuddered, realizing how much it must hurt.

"Over there," Amell nodded into the clearing. It was full daylight, the sun, acting like a glorified spotlight, illuminated a massive structure mounted on a slight rise of land. Like a castle overlooking its fiefdom, the grey concrete maze of buildings towered over the surrounding landscape.

"Wow!" Priya gasped. "It's huge."

"Larger than it appears from this angle," Amell admitted. "And it goes deep underground, too."

"Like Castle Mutasim."

"Mmm!" Amell grunted. "Only much bigger."

"Did you model your castle after this prison?"

"Perhaps, in a way, we all did," came the reply, a tone of remorse etching through his voice. "There's always something about the familiar that makes one feel secure. Even if the familiar is wrought with danger and evil."

Priya nodded in understanding. "So now what?" she asked.

"We wait for the signal," Amell explained. "Then we enter by the main road."

"In broad daylight?" Priya exclaimed. "And we just walk up to the front door and knock?"

"They're expecting us, so, yes."

"Shouldn't we at least wait till night to invade?"

"Never do the obvious when the obvious is expected," Amell advised. "Besides, like I said, they're expecting us."

"Us? As in you and I?" She studied her brother's face intently, seeking answers she knew she wouldn't hear. But, then again, perhaps some of the answers she wouldn't want to hear.

"Yes. Us, as in you and I." Her eyes squinted as if trying to scourge through the outer layer of her brother's skull, to read his mind. She couldn't. She used to be so good at reading Amell's mind. Now, all she drew was a blank. "Are you one of them, Amell? Are you the traitor? Or are you really my brother?" The last thought popped into her head as if planted by someone. Kat? *Kat.* She allowed her mind to reach out for the first time since they left the cave. *Kat. Are you there? Who is this creature who claims to be my brother?*

He is not your brother. Amell is here with me. We're coming. Stall.

The one who claimed to be Amell grabbed Priya's arm, jerking her forward. "Come!" he commanded with brusque intent. "They await. No more communicating with Kat. She can't help you now. Neither can your brother."

"But I can help me." Priya resisted, but the grip was too intense. She kicked out, using all her training from the previous weeks to put up a defense. It was no use. This Amell held tight and merely howled and chortled what might be interpreted as a laugh whenever her foot made contact.

It was her captor's laugh which sent shivers up and down Priya's spine. The creature was no longer pretending to be her brother. Even his appearance was changing, not to a lion as her brother would have done, but into something which resembled more of a wild buffalo, with hooked horns and an evil glint in his eyes. As the grip on her arm tightened, she realized he was holding her in his mouth, the sharp incisors clamping down painfully, barely avoiding breaking her skin.

"What are you?" she shrieked.

"African buffalo," it gargled through clenched teeth, the incisors at least six inches long, and sharp-pointed like nothing Priya had seen in illustrations of wild beasts.

"From Africa. But this is Canada." She thought she detected a shoulder shrug, but she couldn't be sure. She had to do something. Fast. This scenario was getting out of hand. In his favor, not hers. When she noticed a syringe, somehow lodge in the creature's right hoof, she knew it was now or never. She threw back her head and let out the most shrill, ear-piercing scream ever heard on the planet. At least, she hoped it was. The scream rattled the ground beneath them and shook the stunted treetops, as it scattered the few clouds dotting the sky. And, it brought the birds of prey.

She paused in her screaming to take in some air. Noticing the startled look on her aggressor's face, she couldn't resist the quip, "Birds of a feather, flock together." Then she breathed deeply and let her lungs screech ever louder. And they came. Flocks of feathered aggressors. All to her aid. The masses blocked the sun, creating a dome of darkness around Priya and the creature. As she maintained the scream, the birds dove. Hawks and eagles and smaller birds, too. Talons outstretched and beaks open ready to grab and grappled. And it's exactly what they did. In a black cloud they descended on the buffalo creature and tore him to shreds. Piece by bloody piece.

As the creature roared and stomped, swaying its head and horns every which way to block the onslaught, it released the grip on Priya, the syringe rolling away from his hooves. Taking advantage of her freedom, she quickly dove to claim the syringe, before raising her arms and taking flight. Syringe firmly clasped in her right claw, she flew through the thick mass of preying winged creatures, sending out signals of thanks and appreciation to each and every one. Some accompanied her to safety, well within the woods, far from the threatening lab facility. Setting down at the base of a large tree, she resumed her human form, once again thanking her escorts. She allowed her breathing to settle as she took in her surroundings. It was a little clearing, a circle, surrounded by tall trees, guardians of the forest. In the center of the circle was the charred remains of a one-time campfire, protectively situated within another circle, a fire block made of stones.

Pulling her feet closer and crossing them, she noticed the syringe roll away. Not far. Enough to remind her of its potential danger. She reached out and picked it up, clasping her hand around the long arm, not wanting to accidentally poke herself and be injected with whatever lethal dose it held. Holding it carefully, she studied it, trying to determine if it were a sedative or something far worse.

"The cap's on," she whispered to herself, letting out a held breath she hadn't realized she was holding. "That's a relief." She checked the cap and, satisfied it was secure, tucked the syringe in one of the many pockets which lined the legs of her cargo pants. "Who knows when this might come in handy," she reasoned, stretching her legs out again and leaning back against the tree.

She pondered her new life: sometimes human, sometimes owl, sometimes something else. It set the ego aglow, for sure. As she thought of the many changes she'd made, just in the past few days, she started at the realization every time she returned to human form, she was fully dressed.

"How can it be?" she asked herself. Glancing up at the honor guard perched on the treetops surrounding her little piece of safety, she asked them. "Do you know?" All she heard in response was cawing. Shaking her head, she accepted the fact they probably knew less than she did. More questions. But who could she ask? And, for that matter, how did these birds know she needed help? Were they cast-offs from the lab? Set on their own form of revenge for maltreatment within? Questions only led to more questions. The bottom line, however, was these birds had come to her rescue. They had saved her. And now they were standing guard, protecting her.

"Thank you," she cawed skyward. They cawed in response but remained in position. "My honorable guard." She smiled to herself as she allowed her eyes to close. She was safe for now. At least, she hoped she was. Her escort hadn't left, taking up position on various trees around her. They were her winged guard. It was a reassuring sensation. A calming one which allowed her heavy eyelids to droop as exhaustion set in. Two escapes and two threats in one night was more than enough for a seasoned warrior, something Priya was not.

CHAPTER THIRTY-ONE

Voices approached, ever louder, around and inside her head. She was startled awake. Darkness had crept into the woods. She must have slept the day away.

Priya. It was Kat.

Over here, she called back, stifling one yawn after another. She stretched and groaned feeling the muscle aches from all the flying and carrying passengers great distances.

Can you convince your honor guard to stand down?

Priya chuckled. Honor guard indeed. She glanced high into the trees around her secluded resting place. The birds were still there. She felt safe with their presence. Reaching out to them, she called, *Let my friends pass.*

Caw. Caw. Came the gargled response, but the birds remained in place. There was a time when Priya wouldn't have understood their language. She did now.

Reaching out to Kat, she assured her friend, *it's safe. They'll allow your approach.*

Moments later she was embraced in a firm hug, not just from Kat, but her brother as well.

"We thought we'd lost you for good," Kat sniffled.

Amell hugged her tighter. "You did give us quite a scare."

"He looked just like you," Priya argued. "Initially. I should have known when he spoke out against Kat. I shouldn't be so trusting."

"You have a kind heart, little sister," Amell confessed. "You always did."

"I guess it's the elephant in me," she chuckled. "Always passionate to a fault."

"And the chimpanzee and the dolphin," Kat added. "They're extremely friendly and trusting, too."

Priya was really chuckling, now. Others had joined their little group: Roderick and Sassy. "Are these the trusted few?" she asked no one in particular.

"As best we can assume," Amell agreed. "We were about to leave the hideout to launch our assault on the lab, when you disappeared. Then they appeared in droves and we had to evacuate quickly."

"Who was your look-alike?" she had to ask.

"We don't know." Kat took a seat on the ground next to Priya. "There were so many crammed into the cave network. It may have been a transfer from one of the other safe houses. We get them from time to time. We try to screen them, but they have advanced their technology much faster than we have."

"What about the children?" Priya asked in a panic. "Amelie and the others?"

"Safe," Amell assured her.

"They were never housed in the cave complex," Kat confessed. "Remember when you arrived, I disappeared for a long time to tuck Amelie into bed in the children's quarters?" Priya nodded. "Well, it was a bit of trek to the safe house outside the cave. Away from us grownup mutants and the danger we attract. I checked on them quickly after the breach. They're still sound asleep."

"Amelie, too?" After so many stowaway situations with her niece, she wasn't entirely convinced Amelie hadn't found a way to reach Priya.

"Amelie, too. This time, she was way too tired to try anything." Kat chuckled softly. "I'm sure she didn't even know where she was when she did wake up this morning."

"Oh, I don't know," Priya shook her head, still glancing around for her little shadow child. "She is one clever young lady."

Kat pondered Priya's words. "You're right. She is. We can only hope. In the meantime, we have a difficult task ahead of us."

"And we don't want children interfering or causing undo concern amongst us," Amell added, a little more gruffly than he probably intended. But these were stressful times. For all of them.

Amell, Kat and Priya jointed the others as they squatted down on the ground, forming a circle. "Do we attack tonight?" Priya asked, her voice little more than a whisper.

No one answered. The question hung in the air. Perhaps it was unsafe to voice an answer. She had more questions, though. Since everyone was settling in for what might be a prolonged pow-wow of sorts, she decided to assault them all with her questions.

"Amell," she turned to her brother. "Why is it I'm always fully clothed when I return to my human form? Shouldn't my clothes shred in the transformation?"

"Surely you don't want to be naked on your return to human-ness," Roderick teased from across the circle.

Amell cleared his throat. He was preparing to answer when his mate took over. "Have you studied yourself in the alternate forms?" Kat challenged Priya. "I do believe you are mostly transforming inside. Even your owl form only reveals the wings, the talons and a few feathers here and there."

"And the night vision," Priya added.

"Which isn't a visible change," Amell noted, "but definitely a useful tool. You're still wearing your clothes, even as the wings and claws appear. And, thus, they remain when you transform back to your human form." He paused briefly to allow his words to sink in. Then, he added, "I don't think you've ever mastered a complete transformation. Each of your gene mutations are not a dominant gene by any stretch."

Priya nodded, deep in thought. Silence engulfed the space, but only briefly. More questions surfaced. "Why do you suppose the birds came to my rescue and escorted me here? Why are they still standing guard, so to speak? Do you suppose they will follow me into the lab and wreak their own path of destruction?"

Roderick spoke first. "I believe, Priya, your honor guard are former test subjects, lab rats, if you will. They escaped. Somehow. And now they await your advance, our advance, on the common enemy. Them." And he waved his arms dramatically in the general direction of the lab.

"I think Roderick's right, Priya," Kat added her bit. "You called the birds. They came. Rescued you. Now they await your leadership."

"But I'm no leader," Priya protested. "Amell is. Not me."

"Then tell them to follow Amell," Kat suggested. "Either way, they're obviously intent on following our lead. And the more bodies we have to launch our attack, the better."

"And, these birds will be totally unexpected," Sassy pointed out. "Just like your Amell-look-alike was caught off guard, so will 'they' in the lab."

"So, we attack tonight?" Priya asked, allowing her eyes to glance around the circle, night vision allowing her to see everyone as clearly as in daylight, even though the darkness of night was at its thickest in these hours before the moon rose.

"Tonight," the others agreed in unison. The birds in the treetops cawed their consent.

CHAPTER THIRTY-TWO

Amell and Roderick led the discussion, outlining the final details of the planned attack. It was more of a briefing as many of those congregated already knew their role. Amell had insisted on each participant knowing as little as possible until it was time to launch into action. It was safer. More secure. Eliminated possible leaks should someone be captured and compromised.

The details covered, Amell gave the nod to disperse and everyone melted into the darkness of the woods, making way to each individual's allotted spot. Priya held back, wanting a few minutes alone with her brother.

"Amell," she spoke softly. "What about Susan? Will she be joining us?"

"Susan?" he asked, unsure of whom she spoke.

"D'Sonoqua," she whispered, leaning in closer. "The Sasquatch."

"Ah!" Amell responded, understanding his sister's ploy at secrecy. "She'll be there. The Sasquatch are not known as mysterious creatures of the forests for nothing." He wrapped an arm around Priya's shoulder. "Ready?"

"Yes," she agreed. The two walked together in companionable silence, making their way carefully through the forest. When they reached the clearing near the lab complex, Priya spread her wings and set out, leaving her brother behind as she aimed straight for the main entrance. With Amell and Kat on the prowl in their respective lion and cat forms, and the birds of prey flooding the skies all around, Priya flew toward the main entrance, stopping in front of the security cameras before reclaiming human form. She stood there, eyes focused on the entrance, knowing she was covered. Protected. Sort of. As much as one could be protected under the current situation.

"Priya," a monochrome voice bellowed from some sort of loudspeaker. "You may enter." And the massive doors of the main entrance creaked and groaned as they swung toward her, opening the passage into the complex.

Walking slowly, with purpose, Priya made her way forward. Then she stopped. Abruptly. Between the door frames.

"Enter, Priya," the monochrome voice bellowed again. "The doors are about to close."

Priya didn't budge. As she stood there, she heard the creaking doors behind her moving ever closer. If she stayed where she was, she risked being crushed by the impact. Would they allow it? Would they allow their precious creation, her, to be crushed? She was putting them to the test. She held her ground.

And her guardian birds swooped into the enclosure, swarming around her, before slipping into passageways unknown, circling the perimeter of the interior. Missiles projected from strategic positions within the inner compound. Some of the birds were hit. Felled. Most flew on. Still, Priya stood.

"Priya. Enter." The voice was increasingly emphatic.

She stood. The doors groaned to a stop, inches behind her back. Roars from her brother and his mate soared through the space. She lifted her head to join in the chorus and emitted an ear-piercing shriek which summoned more birds of prey until she was clothed in an aura of hovering black masses of feathered friends.

"Priya. Enter." The voice roared, louder than the combined noise of the advancing army of mutants. "You are safe, here, Priya. You were created here. This is where you belong. With us!" As more mutants invaded the inner space, the missiles projected inward at an alarming pace. The ground before Priya was quickly covered with a carpet of multicolored victims.

This was a suicide mission. Horror shivered throughout her body. What had she gotten herself into? Total annihilation of the mutant species? Of life as she was coming to know it? She couldn't back out now. All these creatures who had sacrificed their lives would have died in vain if she backed out.

With renewed vigor, she straightened her spine, pushing back her shoulders, glaring ahead with determination. "No!" her shriek morphed into a singular word, which was drawn out in a lengthy shrill of a high-pitched extension of the vowel. "No!" she re-iterated the consonant, allowing the vowel to transcend again into a lengthy trajectory. She paused. Breathed deeply. Reached down into the side pocket for the only weapon she had: the syringe. She clutched it in one hand, thumb poised, ready to add the pressure which would release its contents. And took one step forward, followed by another. "I enter on my own terms. And I will leave of my own accord." She was snarling, now. "Come out and show yourself. Whoever you are."

She made her way to the center of the entry space. The doors behind her clanged to a close once she had released her position barricading the process. "Come out!" she yelled, allowing her head to search up and down and all around, seeking someone, something to indicate what or who was in control.

Another set of doors opened at the far end of the room. Priya remained rooted where she stood. "Enter, Priya. And you shall have your answers."

Mesmerized, she took another step forward.

A lone figure, draped in a white robe (prophetic, perhaps, but certainly not reassuring) appeared in the center of the doorway leading into the void. A hand reached forward, beckoning Priya. She felt a tug, as if someone else controlled her motions. She took yet another step.

"Stop!" she heard Amell's voice snarl.

Stop! Kat whispered the same inside her head.

Why? She sent her message to Kat.

Trap door in the floor. One more step and you'll fall into a cavernous pit and be trapped in their lair of deceit.

Like a lab rat.

And worse.

Priya stopped.

"Come closer, child," the voice beckoned. It was hypnotic. She wasn't sure if it came from the figure standing in the far doorway or from somewhere far deeper within the compound. The tone echoed and ricocheted around the space. Enticing. Luring. She wanted to obey. To take another step. And another. But she held back.

Out of the corner of her eyes, she noticed Amell and Kat circling the outer regions of the space. Staying well away from the center. Away from the danger. But, was there danger? Kat sensed her turmoil. Picking up a random object, she tossed it to the center of the ground, mere steps in front of Priya. A cavern opened and the object disappeared with a perceptible woosh. Startled, Priya stepped back.

"You tricked me. You deceived me. This is not my home. It was never my home and never will be. You can't make me come. You can't use me as you've used so many others." She ranted on and on, taking another step back. The door behind her had long since closed. There was no escape. She could go forward and risk plunging into the trap. She could stay standing where she was, hurling verbal insults. Or she could follow Kat's path, or Amell's, and proceed with caution around the perimeter. She chose Kat's path, keeping her eyes rivetted on the figure who continued to stand, like a statue, the only movement being the hand which beckoned.

"Come, child. Come." The voice droned on.

"No!" she challenged. "You come out here." Her eyes focused on the opening space behind the figure. It was dark. Void. Not a welcoming space by any stretch of the imagination.

"Priya. Enter."

"No!" They were at a stalemate. And then the roars and shrieks and all manner of threatening wild sounds erupted both within and without the enclosure.

She held firm. "No!" she screamed, scrunching her eyes shut and forcing her head to turn away from the pulling force. She raised her hands, palms forward, in front of her as a shield, her grip on the syringe loosening, but not entirely. She felt the drag in spite of her efforts to control it, but she held on, clearing her mind of all things except the ensuing battle.

Others around her were similarly fighting the force, struggling to maintain control of their space, of their position, of their power to assault the enemy.

"Nooooo!" Priya screamed with an impassioned drawing out of the vowel. And her remaining force, birds of prey of all sizes, flooded the entryway, darkening what little light there was. The robed figure took a step back. The beckoning power lessened. Priya felt the release and took advantage of it. As did the others. She spread her arms and jumped into the air, her arms becoming wings as she took flight, leading the charge. "Now!" she commanded, both verbally and through her thoughts. She led the invading force forward, intent on attacking the lone figure before he managed to close the entrance, an act he appeared to be preparing to do. His motions were fast when he noticed the imminent assault, but not fast enough.

Priya plunged headfirst into the voice. Her mouth, now a pointed beak, met its target, piercing the upper portion of the robed figure, presumably its head. "No!" It was the figure's turn to protest, to shelter itself with limbs. Too little. Too late. Priya dropped to the floor and, wings folding as they faded, jabbed the syringe into the figure at the nearest point, plunging the contents with unnecessary force until there was no more plunging capacity. The figure crumbled to the floor, with one final, feeble protest, "No!"

The others entered the space around her, the bird protective force hovering close by, while Amell, Kat, Roderick and the remaining troopers from Castle Mutasim pressed deeper into the facility. As figures moved, more lights glowed, illuminating the corridors leading, presumably, to lab rooms and places of confinement, the cages. Creatures could be heard beckoning the invaders, some pleading for release, others shouting commands in an attempt to control the invaders. Whatever devices had once been planted in Priya's head, and the others, had either been removed or had lost their ability to override and take control. The invaders were in control.

As they made progress within, shrieks and thumping could be heard from the forests behind them. The Sasquatch had arrived. The back-up plan. Would they be needed? It didn't matter, they were a part of this onslaught. They had invested hatred for the facility and all who worked therein. Susan and the others would trample and destroy everything and anything in their path to grind out for eternity the horrors which had been inflicted on them and their kind for centuries.

While Priya stood guard over her victim, waiting to assure herself it was incapacitated or, possibly, dead, the others crashed through one door after another, setting off alarms, releasing locks and allowing creatures of all sizes and shapes to emerge into the foray of imminent disaster. More robed figures scurried around, but they were now the victims, as their lab subjects took revenge, tearing one after the other apart, limb by limb.

CHAPTER THIRTY-THREE

"Stop!" Priya didn't know where the voice came from, but she had a feeling it was hers. "Stop! Enough!" She picked her feet up higher than usual to prevent stumbling over the carnage, the blood and gore carpeting the floor causing her to slip. Fortunately, she maintained her footing and carried on, deeper into the facility. "Stop!" she continued to shriek, her voice gaining volume as bile threatened at the back of her throat. She didn't like this. Not one bit. It was one thing for these creatures to experiment on her and the others. It was wrong. It was quite another for her band of mutants to turn totally rogue and tear everything apart, living and not-quite-alive. Some of the mutants had been released from their cages and were joining in the battle. These biological creations had no self control, no remorse for what they did. They killed and disembowelled anyone in their path, their captors and rescuers alike. It was, quite simply, a blood bath. And it had to end.

"Stop!" A stronger voice joined hers. It was Amell. He stepped up beside Priya, disheveled and plastered with human and inhuman remains. "Enough!" Kat joined them. And Roderick. Then, out of the far end of the hall, a passageway opened, where once there had been only a wall. And more creatures marched through. Fully armed. With Wayne leading the way.

"Wayne!" Priya shrieked. She would have run forward, if Kat hadn't taken her elbow and held her back.

"No, Priya," she half snarled. "It's not Wayne. Not the Wayne you know, anyway."

She was right. Behind Wayne an entire battalion of Wayne's followed. They were not mere mutants, but clones. Or, worse, robots? Priya couldn't be sure. Wayne's army took up position along the far end of the hall, and took aim: toward Priya and her group, toward the rampaging mobs in the various lab rooms lining the hall. Silence replaced the noise of destruction as the invaders suddenly took stock and realized they were doomed.

A now familiar shriek shattered the still air, echoing along the clinical hallways, rattling anything and everything which remained standing. The floors shook and even the programmed attack squad glanced around warily. There was no evidence of the source of the shrieks, of the approaching creatures who rattled the facility. And, then, every wall along the corridor crumbled as one Sasquatch after another barged through, Susan taking the lead.

As she stormed past, she yelled, "I have your back, Amell. I have your back."

Wayne and his look-alikes didn't stand a chance. Even the backup Wayne-army marching in droves after the lead Wayne crumbled under foot didn't stand a chance. They were knocked flat like weak little dominoes, one after another. The Sasquatch trampled on those who fell, plummeting their bodies into those who didn't.

"And the moral of the story is don't create what you can't control," Amell quipped. He was referring to the Sasquatches as much as all the other mutant creations.

And then it was over. An eery silence entombed the aftershocks which rattled through the facility. Amell grabbed Priya's arm, steering her further down the hall. "We have to get the records before our invaders destroy them as well," he explained.

Kat, two steps behind, explained, "We need the records to study what they did in the hopes of reversing, or at least, putting a permanent stop to what they began."

Priya nodded in understanding as they approached the one remaining door which barred entry. Amell released his hold on Priya and barged against the door with all his body force. It didn't budge. Sounds could be heard on the other side.

"They're in there," Kat sniffed around the floor near the door. "They're destroying their work. We must be quick."

"But how?" Priya asked.

"Only you can do it, Priya," Amell explained, pointing to the square pad next to the door. "It's activated by a handprint. Yours will work."

"Mine?" she exclaimed. "Why mine?"

"Because our father was one of them," he pointed viciously toward the door and those who presumably stood on the other side. "He created this means of entry. Only a half-dozen hands can activate the mechanism and unlock the door. And yours is one of those hands."

"But I don't understand why my hand would work when yours and the others won't." Priya took a step back, wanting to distance herself from the possibility she was one of them. "No," she shook her head, trembling from head to foot. "It can't be."

"Priya," Amell approached her and gently took hold of her shoulders. "Priya," he repeated. "Our father amputated his right hand and had it implanted on you. It happened during the surgery you don't remember, when they supposedly removed your tonsils. Your hand was, is, our father's hand."

"Ich!" she grimaced, giving her right hand a good shake as if it would help dislodge it from her body. Realization dawned on her. She gasped, glancing furtively between her brother and his mate. "Is that why they were so desperate to capture me?"

"Partially," Amell admitted. "They wouldn't want you to fall in with us. When they noticed we were getting close to you, they increased their efforts to control you. I'm assuming there was something in the mechanisms implanted in your brain that countered many of their controlling methods. Hence the appearance of your friend Sammy and the man who almost became your boyfriend, what was his name?"

"Maurice," Priya replied automatically, cringing at the memories which threatened to surface. She glanced at her brother, then at Kat, and back at her brother, shivering at all that had transpired. And for what? Money? Power? Control? It all seemed so pointless. "I suppose Wayne was also their spy right from the beginning."

She was surprised when Amell shook his head. "We don't think so," he spoke in a soothing tone. "We believe he was abducted and replaced sometime immediately before your accident. Cloned. His original may well be somewhere in this facility."

She cleared her throat and braced her shoulders. "Then I'd better make use of father's hand and get us inside so we can find out. Before it's too late. For Wayne and for all the others."

She palm-planted the screen and it illuminated with a distinct humming sound. A latch clicked and the door swung open. Releasing her contact, she stepped into the room and gasped. Creatures of all size and description hustled around, smashing devices and pocketing what appeared to be memory cards. They barely paused when she walked into the room followed by the others. At the far end, one of the taller creatures glanced at her and straightened his shoulders. It reached his hands forward and electrified sparks emitted from the tips of what might be identified as fingers. The sparks slithered across the counter surfaces separating them, smouldering every electronic device in its path, gaining momentum and power as it approached Priya's gathered invaders. It wasn't a sharp, brisk motion, as one would expect with an energy source which sizzled like lightning. Rather, it was slow and contained. As if it were soaking up, absorbing everything in its path.

Automatically, Priya held up her father's hand, palm toward the approaching threat. The sparks, attracted to the palm, sunk deep into the folds of the skin, dissipating and fizzling out.

Why did you do that? Kat whispered inside her head. *How did you know?*

Priya merely shrugged her shoulders.

"Priya," bellowed the creature who sourced the sparks. "Daughter of the traitor, Rohan Agarwal. And your brother, Amell Agarwal. Another traitor. I should have had you destroyed at birth. Both of you."

"Who and what are you?" Priya demanded.

The creature barred his shoulders, standing even straighter. Holding her gaze, he announced, "I am Purab Kshatriya. Of course, that's only my given name for earthlings. My real name is Brsptolgrapolongiiiiii. Where I come from, it means All Powerful One."

"Humph!" Amell grunted from where he stood blocking the open doorway.

"And where do you come from?" Priya asked.

"Mengelea." The response was brief. "Far across the galaxy. We are Mengelean medicalizers. Supreme scientists who have the ability to create the most powerful living creatures on this planet and many others."

"No more!" Priya made herself stand proud to meet his glare face on. "We come to put an end to this insanity."

"Do you, now?" Purab snarled in response. "And how do you propose to do that?"

Once again, Priya had no control over the hand which wasn't hers. It raised on its own accord and, palm forward, took aim at Purab. Sparks flew across the space between them, hitting the target in multiple locations. Purab let out a shriek, making a futile attempt to barricade itself from the onslaught. It was neither fast nor effective enough to dull the impact. The figure of the antagonist smouldered, withered and crumbled in a puddle, partially on the table before slithering to the floor.

The other creatures in the room froze; their actions incapacitated by the loss of the leader, for it was obvious Purab had been the leader of the pack. Amell and the others swarmed the room, taking charge. Memory cards were secured, what few remained, and computer monitors and technical devices barricaded from the enemy before further damage could be inflicted. Purab's followers were herded out into the hall where the demolition continued. Amell gave strict orders to guard the survivors as their intel would be useful. His orders fell on deaf ears as the pent-up anger of those abused and mutilated exploded on the remaining Mengelean medicalizers.

"They were no better than the Nazis," Priya muttered under her breath.

Kat came forward to stand next to her, placing a soothing arm around Priya's shoulder. "They are what remains of the Nazis," she explained. Noticing the surprised expression, she nodded, "They created and perpetuated the madness of Mengele and his medical experiments. Not only did they kill and annihilate entire populations, but they also created horrendous creatures for their goal of mass destruction. This here," she waved her other hand around, "this is only one of many labs around the world. We may have won the battle here, but the war is yet to be won."

"Amell. Kat. Priya," Roderick called from the far end of the room. He was monitoring a screen which depicted images of caged creatures, some part human.

The trio joined Roderick and studied the images on the screen. "There must be another room we haven't checked. With a hidden passage."

"How did this monitor remain untouched in their scourging?" Amell asked.

Roderick merely shrugged his shoulders. "Perhaps they felt a need to continue watching the creatures in this secluded room in case it was compromised. But look here." He flicked the touchscreen and the image zoomed into one cage.

"Wayne!" Priya gasped. "But…"

"Perhaps the original," Roderick suggested. "The others we knew were clones. Perhaps all the Waynes you encountered were clones."

"But…" Her hands flew to her face, covering her anguish. She allowed tears to trickle unchecked down her cheeks. "So, I never knew the real Wayne? He won't know me."

"You may have known the real Wayne," Amell said calmly as he wrapped his arm around Priya's shoulder. "The story the Wayne at Castle Mutasim shared about their invasion. Perhaps he was switched at that point."

"So, he might know me," Priya sniffled, rubbing her nose and cheeks with the cuff of her sleeve. "If he remembers anything at all, that is. He's all consumed with tubes. Immobilized. Frozen in time and place. What now?"

"We must find this lab room," Roderick responded. "There's creatures in there as well, set to destroy before we can conquer. We must move with haste."

"I agree," Amell concurred. "Any suggestions?"

"There's a lower level," Roderick noted. "We found the access behind a hidden door. Before we invaded this room. The troops are down there now. Hopefully not destroying everything in their path. Come. I'll show you." He led Priya, Amell and Kat out of the control room, once they were satisfied things were being properly preserved and protected. Amell assigned guards at the entrance and hastened after the others.

The entrance to a staircase leading downward was indeed well concealed. A single panel had once covered the entrance, presumably activated in a similar manner to the entrance to the control room. This one had been totally destroyed, the invaders intent on accessing every space to destroy and conquer all.

The stairs were narrow, spiralling in a tight circular pattern, much like the one at Castle Mutasim, the one Kat had reluctantly led Priya down into the secret labs beneath the castle.

Kat held back, not caring to venture downward. "I'll wait up here." She shuddered noticeably. "Make sure no one interferes."

No one commented. The remaining trio were well aware of Kat's phobia about deep, dark places. She was an above-ground type of person, or cat. They left Kat at her post and made the steep descent. Lights illuminated, picking up heat sensors as they approached a specific part of the stairwell, brightening like a spotlight, zeroing in on their bodies, following their progress. It was eery, unnerving, but the group moved on.

It was a lengthy descent. Priya was feeling waves of dizziness as they walked around in circles, each step taking them lower into the sub-structure of the complex. Finally, their feet met a firm platform, each one breathing a sigh of relief. It was brief. Glancing around, they noted the rockface walls which allowed them barely enough space to move. There was no apparent opening or break in the wall to suggest a hidden passageway.

"I thought you said others were down here," Amell accused Roderick.

"They were," he said in his defense. "Perhaps they couldn't proceed and gave up down here."

"Or perhaps they made access through some hidden panel which shuttered closed after they passed through," Priya suggested.

"Perhaps," the two men pondered aloud in unison.

Taking charge of the situation, Amell told them, in a quiet tone only meant for their ears, "Feel around the walls. Priya touch each stone at various intervals. There must be a hidden passage somewhere. Why else the hidden stairs leading down here?"

Roderick made his way in one direction while Priya felt around the opposite direction. Amell studied the floor stones. Priya met Roderick at the half-way point and was about to give up, since the other half had been surveyed, but Roderick insisted she continue. After all, she did have the hand, her father's hand, which could open unknown spaces. "There must be something I missed," he said with marginal encouragement. "You'll be able to find it if there's anything to find."

And so she continued, pausing briefly before a rock which appeared to jut outward. She ran her hand over it, feeling for some sort of device. Finding nothing, she shrugged her shoulders and was about to move on when she stopped. This rock hadn't appeared before. She and Roderick would have noticed it. Wouldn't they? Placing her father's hand on the rock, she pressed firmly, as if to push it back into the rockface wall. Nothing happened at first, then, a shuddering rattled the floor beneath them and, where there had only been a rock wall, there was now an opening to a passageway.

"Priya." Amell walked up to his sister and placed a hand gently on her shoulder. "You lead the way. Feel along the walls on both sides as you go. This passageway has to lead to more labs. I shudder at what we'll find down here."

As if she were soaking in his unease, Priya shuddered as she nodded her head in agreement. Without a word, she took the first step into the passageway. It was dark, like the stairs had been, until she stepped forward. She felt like she was walking onto a darkened stage and then the spotlight was upon her. Placing the right hand on the wall, she allowed it to trail along with her, matching step for step. She jumped when the first door literally popped open, revealing a void of beeping machines holding creatures within. There were no controlling bodies, so Amell urged her on. They'd return later to study and release the victims, if possible.

The passageway came to an abrupt end. Nothing opened. Priya felt all around the blocking wall. Nothing. She let out a primal cry and felt around more frantically. Until she sensed a warm pulsation. She pressed firmly on the spot and the wall evaporated before them. Stepping across the threshold, she let out a shriek which vibrated across the chambers lining the passageway. Controlling creatures of all shapes and sizes froze in their tracks as she marched in, followed by Amell and Roderick. In the center of the room was a glass-encased edifice, larger than life. Fluids bubbled within and a figure stood glaring out at them.

"Wayne! Bear! No!" She shrieked louder, calling out his name over and over again. She tried to surge forward, to somehow release the Wayne she thought she knew from his bondage. Amell and Roderick held her back. Finally, she crumpled against Amell, her head buried into his shoulder as she sobbed herself to oblivion.

CHAPTER THIRTY-FOUR

She must have passed out. When she regained consciousness, she was in her room. The one at Castle Mutasim. But it couldn't be, could it? The castle had been destroyed. She let out a groan and struggled to sit up. She scrunched her eyes shut and opened them again, surveying the space around her. It was her room at Castle Mutasim.

"Ah! You're awake. Finally." It was Kat. She walked across the room, sleekly, as only a cat could do and perched on the side of Priya's bed. "You gave us quite a scare. Again. Susan carried you here."

"Susan? The Sasquatch? D'Sonoqua?"

Kat laughed. "One and the same. And your sister." She noticed Priya's eyes darting around the room. "You recognize the space? And you're full of questions? Mostly how? Well," she slapped hands on her knees and gave a cheekiest grin. "You are at Castle Mutasim. The real one. Your things were moved over before the other castle was demolished. You probably didn't notice anything missing the last time you were in your room. We can be quite enigmatic when needed. Which is most of the time." She let out a cat-ish giggle.

Kat's giggle was infectious. Or, perhaps, it was comic relief to join in the laughter. Which she did. And she didn't understand why. With a cough, she brought her outburst under control. Sort of. And asked, "But my things were also in my assigned room in the underground safe place. How?"

Another giggle. "We have ways of duplicating things. Our team worked hard to make it appear like your room. Your space. Your things. Most were duplicates. Others, like your journal, were whisked from one safe place to the next."

"And all is here?" Priya asked, running her hand along the side of the bed, searching for her hidden journal. Finding it, she pulled it out, and randomly flipped through the pages, searching for her last entry. It was there. Just as she'd written. "Did you read it?"

"No." Kat held up her hands in mock defense. "I wouldn't do that. I have enough to consider merely reading your mind. And the minds of others, too."

"I suppose." She replaced the journal, pulling the covers down to conceal its hiding place. Not that it mattered, now, since Kat, and who knows who else, knew where she hid it. With a sigh, she glanced at her brother's mate. "So, where are we? Really?"

"Castle Mutasim. I told you."

"Yes, but where?"

"All in good time."

"And Wayne? What happened to Wayne? And the others?"

"Come. Get dressed. We'll join the others." Before Priya could protest and demand more answers to her questions, Kat had slipped out of the room, closing the door behind her.

Alone, Priya pondered her memories of the attack. They had found Wayne. Encased in some device which monitored and controlled his entire being, presumably keeping him alive to create more cells to clone. She shuddered at the memory. How could a living creature do such a thing to another living creature? And why? Who were these creatures anyway?

Shaking her head, she threw back the covers and swung her legs over the side of the bed. Noticing some track pants and a pullover sweater lying over the chair near the bed, she grabbed them and made her way to the bathroom to quickly wash and dress. She needed answers. And she wanted them. Now.

The hall outside her room was empty and quiet as a tomb. She made her way to the top of the stairs and gingerly began her descent. Raised voices drew her down to the main level before veering off toward the large living room, where she and the others frequently gathered in the evening to discuss the day's events or just unwind with a book, a game or a puzzle.

"We can't tell her!" It was Roderick. She knew his voice well. As she did most of the others. It was her sensitive hearing which helped her identify different sounds like the tonal quality of an individual's voice. She stepped into the room, pausing a mere step beyond the threshold. Roderick and Amell were faced off in the center, obviously in the middle of heated discussion. They hadn't noticed her entrance. Kat had. She cleared her throat in a vain attempt to get their attention. It didn't work. At least not before Priya had her say.

"You can't tell me what?" she demanded, glaring first at her brother and then at Roderick.

Both stepped back from the other, eyes downcast like guilty little boys caught in the act of doing something they knew they shouldn't do.

Amell cleared his throat and spoke first, "Priya." He cleared his throat again before allowing his eyes to rise until they met hers. "You're up. You look much better."

"Better than what?" Priya asked, coyly raising one eyebrow as if in a challenge. "And what is it you can't tell me?"

It was Roderick who cleared his throat this time. "That Wayne is no longer Wayne. And, as soon as we disconnect him, he will die."

Priya felt deflated, stepping back as if putting some distance between herself and the others would change the facts. She was shaking her head to negate the news. Neither worked. Fact was fact, after all. Kat had wrapped an arm around Priya's shoulders, to comfort, to protect in case she fainted. Again. She'd have to put a stop to this fainting. And there'd be no fainting now. She had to know the truth. She had to see Wayne.

"Priya." Amell's hands flew up to ward off argument, "It's what he wants. That is, after he's had a chance to see you. To talk to you. To explain."

She breathed deeply, pondering her brother's words. Finally, she nodded. "Very well. Where is he?"

"In the labs. Below."

This castle was indeed like the previous one. Complete with hidden labs and high-tech devices. To study. To protect.

Turning to leave, Priya held up her hands to stop others from following. "I know the way," she said. "I need to do this on my own."

Amell, ever the stubborn, over-protective brother, stepped forward in spite of her protests. "I'll escort you to the room where they're keeping him alive. Then, I'll leave you two alone and wait in the hall in case you need me or want my presence. I'm not allowing you to go alone, Priya."

She studied his face, his eyes betraying concern. "You think he might be imbedded with some sort of controlling device that will infect me?"

Amell merely shrugged.

"I suppose anything's possible," she answered her own challenge.

The two made their way to the rear of the castle and descended the lengthy staircase into the deepest depths below. Lights illuminated the path before and behind as their footsteps clattered on metal steps before reaching the firm stone base at the bottom. Amell led Priya down the hall, pausing in front of a door, the same door which opened to the same room Sammy had occupied before she self-terminated. But that had been another Castle Mutasim. This one was fully intact.

Her brother noticed Priya hesitate. He knew. He understood. "It's not the same, Priya." He didn't wait for a response, opening the door to a room which pulsated with pumps and monitors and the distinguished sound of flushing fluids.

"I know." She took a deep breath, braced her shoulders and stepped across the threshold.

Amell waved the single occupant into the hall. The door whooshed closed behind her and Priya was alone. At least, she was the only creature, human or otherwise, who stood on the firm floor of the lab. The other living being was encased in the fluid-filled glass casket as he had been at the lab facility. Numerous tubes encased the body, poking in and out at various intervals. Only the eyes were fully visible; the mouth, nose and ears sported monstrous tubes dangling like earrings.

"Priya." The voice was garbled as one would expect from someone speaking under water. It was definitely Wayne's voice, though. "Forgive me."

She stood frozen; feet rooted to the floor. She could barely breathe. Why was this affecting her so much? Wayne had deceived her. She shouldn't be caring, compassionate. Forgiving? Shuddering at the flashback to the scene in the clearing when they almost captured her. With his assistance. Taking a step forward, tentatively, she steeled herself against the emotions, conflicting and sincere, which cascaded through her senses.

"You deceived me, Wayne," she accused him, coming to a full stop within arm's length from the tomb which encased him. "Why, Wayne? Why?"

"They made me do it, Priya." His voice, gargled, betrayed a whine of despair. "They made me do it. Even now, they control me. They promise me release from this prison, but really, they only want me to control you. So, they can control you."

Priya fought the urge to step back, even as she noticed Wayne's arms raise in spite of the tubes which engulfed his body like a shroud from head to toe. "Why, Wayne? Why do they want me so bad?"

"Because you are their ultimate creation, Priya," he sputtered. His body gave a violent shudder, as if he were fighting the inner workings which were enforcing their control on all he did and spoke. "You…" he was about to say more, when a wail escaped his lips and his arms flailed recklessly. The glass tomb shattered, and he stepped out with ease, eyes glowing red, tubes fluttering around him like loose feathers. "Priya." It was no longer Wayne's voice, but rather something unearthly. "Priya. Come to us."

She stepped back, assessed the approaching zombie-like creature and screamed. Amell was beside her within minutes as she continued to watch in horror the growing power as it approached.

"Priya," it called. It was no longer Wayne. It was no longer human. Nor was it a mutant. It no longer was a breathing creature.

Others rushed in behind them, bearing weapons.

"No!" Priya held her hands in a vain attempt to stop the attack.

We have no choice, Priya. Kat spoke quietly in her head. She and the others had joined them in the deeply buried caverns of the complex. In spite of her request, they stand down. Stay away. They had come. *We had to come, Priya. We didn't know what Wayne could or would do. Now, we have no choice. You know that.*

Priya took another step back, allowing Kat, who had stepped in the room, to wrap arms around her shoulders, turning her away from the approaching carnage. As the two left the room, shrieks and explosions erupted. The last thing Priya heard was the earth-shattering scream, "Priya."

"Priya." She paused to watch Roderick dash out into the courtyard. He trotted toward her, a huge grin on his face. Approaching her side, he took a hand in his and walked forward. "Let's walk. And talk."

It had been six months since the demolishing of the lab facility in northern Alberta. Since the destruction of the other Castle Mutasim and the annihilation of all the Waynes, including the original Wayne. Priya needed every minute of those six months to recover. In less than a year, she had experienced a total upheaval in her life, coming to terms with the fact she wasn't human. Or, at least, not totally human. A mutant. A freak. With nightly treks soaring through the night air in an owl form and daily workouts in the gym to strengthen her other genetic powers, she was beginning to feel invincible. And, best yet, a part of the Castle Mutasim family.

The two walked in companionable silence around the perimeter of the castle ramparts. It was Roderick who broke the silence. "You know Amell is leaving?" It was half question, half statement.

Priya nodded sadly. "Another castle to build and another lab to exterminate." She wasn't bitter. Not really. She knew it was Amell's calling. It made her sad, though. She had only recently reconnected with her brother and now he was about to disappear from her life. Again. And, of course, Kat and their children would be going, too. She wasn't too happy to be losing her little shadow, Amelie. But perhaps it was for the best, as Amelie had a tendency to get herself into dire predicaments when attempting to follow her aunt.

"Will you go with him?" Roderick asked.

Priya was startled. She had considered the possibility. Especially when Amell asked her to join them. He had also asked her to stay. To take care of Castle Mutasim. To be at the helm, so to speak, taking his place while he was elsewhere. Either possibility was wrought with stress and fears of incompetence. "I don't know," she answered honestly, pulling up short. "I feel as if I belong here. Amell trusts me to take care of the castle. His castle."

"I'd like you to come," Roderick announced with almost forced bluntness. "Amell asked me to join them. I told him I wouldn't consider it without you."

Priya blushed. Coughing to hide a sudden set of nerves, she said, "Amell needs you at his side, Roderick. You must go. With or without me."

He gripped her hand more firmly, tugging gently to nestle her body next to his. "I suppose," he agreed reluctantly. "Couldn't Susan take the helm? She's done well over the years keeping the Sasquatch in line."

"She's already returned to her cave." Priya had developed a close bond with her sister. In spite of their differences, and because of them, they forged a relationship based on respect and common goals. She hated to see Susan leave the castle, to return to the wild. But she knew she'd see her again. It was inevitable. The war wasn't over yet. They'd only won the first battle. She patted Roderick's arm reassuringly. "I will be here when you return."

"So, you have decided?"

She nodded. "I think so. I'm needed here more than elsewhere. And I need to set down roots, to start feeling safe and content with where I am. And, more important, who I am."

He nodded with a mixture of compassion and understanding. "I'll miss you, Priya."

"And I you."

The sky darkened as the sun faded into the horizon. Feeling the blackness engulf them, Priya felt the urge to take flight. It was the nocturnal nature of her owl gene. Roderick understood. He sensed her growing restlessness. "Go, Priya," he commanded softly. Before releasing her hand, he pulled her into a tight embrace and kissed her soundly on the lips. Breathless, they pulled apart. "Go and soar the night skies. I'll be gone when you return. But we will meet again."

Priya stepped back, blending into the blackness of night. Spreading her arms, she felt the feathers surge forth giving her wings. Taking off, she soared mere feet above where she had left Roderick. He only glanced once, waved, then he, too, faded into the night. She soared higher, in broader circles, then took off into the night sky over the forest, seeking her feathered friends and a night of reckless abandon. Seeking the beauty embedded deep within every living creature. The beauty within the beast.

About the Author

Emily-Jane Hills Orford has fond memories and lots of stories that evolved from a childhood growing up in a haunted Victorian mansion. Told she had a 'vivid imagination', the author used this talent to create stories in her head to pass tedious hours while sick, waiting in a doctor's office, listening to a teacher drone on about something she already knew, or enduring the long, stuffy family car rides. The author lived her stories in her head, allowing her imagination to lead her into a different world, one of her own making. As the author grew up, these stories, imaginings and fantasies took to the written form and, over the years, she developed a reputation for telling a good story. Emily-Jane can now boast that she is an award-winning author of several books, including *Queen Mary's Daughter* (Clean Reads 2018), *Gerlinda* (CFA 2016) which received an Honorable Mention in the 2016

Readers' Favorite Book Awards, *To Be a Duke* (CFA 2014) which was named Finalist and Silver Medalist in the 2015 Next Generation Indie Book Awards and received an Honorable Mention in the 2015 Readers' Favorite Book Awards and several other books.

A retired teacher of music and creative writing, she writes about the extraordinary in life and the fantasies of dreams combined with memories. For more information on the author, check out her website at:

http://emilyjanebooks.ca